"No! This

Vittorio said fierce

"Why must I go?" Melanie murmured.

"Why? Because you are so beautiful that I cannot look at you without wanting to touch you. I forget that some things are impossible."

"Nothing is impossible," she said recklessly.

He laughed mirthlessly. "It's only in fairy tales that the frog becomes a prince. Once I could have fought for you and made you mine. Now I haven't even the right to think of it."

"Then why did you kiss me that night?" she demanded. "Did that *have* to be?"

"Yes, it had to be. We couldn't know each other without that happening. You know that's true . . . you felt it the first moment . . . as I did."

"The first moment—but not only then. You shouldn't have kissed me if you didn't mean this to happen."

His mouth twisted. "You're right to reproach me. I couldn't stop myself then."

"And now you can?"

"I must. I called you *fiore di fuòco*. It means fire flower. And I've known you were the fire flower from the beginning."

Dear Reader:

Welcome to Silhouette Desire – provocative, compelling, contemporary love stories written by and for today's woman. These are stories to treasure.

Each and every Silhouette Desire is a wonderful romance in which the emotional and the sensual go hand in hand. When you open a Desire, you enter a whole new world – a world that has, naturally, a perfect hero just waiting to whisk you away! A Silhouette Desire can be light-hearted or serious, but it will always be satisfying.

We hope you enjoy this Desire today – and will go on to enjoy many more.

Please write to us:

Jane Nicholls
Silhouette Books
PO Box 236
Thornton Road
Croydon
Surrey
CR9 3RU

LUCY
GORDON

THE SICILIAN

Silhouette Desire

Originally Published by Silhouette Books
a division of
Harlequin Enterprises Ltd.

*First published in Great Britain in 1991
by Silhouette Books, Eton House, 18-24 Paradise Road,
Richmond, Surrey TW9 1SR*

© Lucy Gordon 1991

Silhouette, Silhouette Desire and Colophon are
Trade Marks of Harlequin Enterprises B.V.

ISBN 0 373 58249 8

22 – 9108

Made and printed in Great Britain

LUCY GORDON

met her husband-to-be in Venice, fell in love the first evening and got engaged two days later. After seventeen years they're still happily married and now live in England with their three dogs. For twelve years Lucy was a writer on an English women's magazine. She interviewed many of the world's most interesting men, including Warren Beatty, Richard Chamberlain, Roger Moore, Sir Alec Guinness and Sir John Gielgud.

Other Silhouette Books by Lucy Gordon

Silhouette Desire

Take All Myself
The Judgement of Paris
A Coldhearted Man
My Only Love, My Only Hate
A Fragile Beauty
Just Good Friends
Eagle's Prey
For Love Alone
Vengeance is Mine
Convicted of Love

Silhouette Special Edition

Legacy of Fire
Enchantment in Venice
Bought Woman

One

When she first saw him through the blinding Sicilian sun, she thought he was a mirage. Then she realized this was the result of heat haze, floating up in shimmering waves of air from the baked surfaces of the airport. The real man was just above medium height, with the sturdy, muscular build of the southern Italian. He wore thin cotton trousers that ended halfway down his calves, and the heat caused them to cling damply to his thighs and loins, outlining every muscle, every smooth, curved surface. His chest was covered by an olive-green sleeveless vest, and he wore old sandals.

He came toward her. "Lady Melanie Carlyle?" he asked.

"That's right."

"I am Vittorio Farnese." He looked at the trolley on which her luggage was piled. "Do you have all your bags here?'' He spoke English with an accent, but smoothly, without having to hunt for words.

"Yes, this is everything."

"Then I will take them."

She followed him to a battered Jeep in the parking lot, where he tossed her heavy bags into the trunk as though they were featherlight. She gasped at the heat. Only a few hours ago she'd been in England, where the sun was a gentle friend. Here the light had a brilliant, savage harshness that crashed against her as if trying to drive her into the earth.

"Get inside," Vittorio said, "or that pale, northern skin will make you suffer."

He glanced over her slender, small-boned frame and frowned. Melanie was used to strangers mistakenly thinking her fragile. She was of medium height, but seemed taller because of the self-confidence that had been bred into her. Born twenty-seven years ago into one of the oldest titled families in England, she'd soon learned to face the world with her head up and a touch of queenliness in her bearing.

Background apart, she attracted homage through her delicate blond beauty that made her look almost ethereal. It came as a shock to people to discover that her elegant hands could control a recalcitrant horse, that she could walk all day through muddy countryside without tiring, and that her fine features and soft curving mouth hid a will of iron.

As she got into the Jeep and sat fanning herself, she was calling upon all her determination to hide the fact that she was already wilting in the heat. Perhaps Harris had been right all along. He'd advised her not to come to Sicily. "There's no need for it, darling," he'd insisted.

"Just tell the lawyer to sell the estate and send you the money."

"But I'd like to see my inheritance before I dispose of it," she'd argued.

"I don't see the point. The lawyer says Pietro Salvani has offered a fair price, so what's the problem?"

"I want to see what became of Dulcie," was all Melanie could say, and this answer had made Harris stare.

"But you know what became of her," he expostulated. "She visited Sicily, lost her head and married a farmer. Now she's dead. What else is there to know?"

"Perhaps I want to know how a sensible woman like Dulcie *came* to lose her head," Melanie mused, unable to define it further, even to herself.

In her childhood she'd known her Aunt Dulcie well. She still had a clear picture of her: middle-aged, good-looking in a slightly forbidding way, unmarried and a pillar of the community. She bred dogs, ran the youth club, was on several charity committees and took no interest in her appearance unless she was making herself tidy for church. But when Melanie was fourteen, Dulcie—dear, dull, dependable Dulcie—had gone on holiday to Sicily and never returned. Melanie's father visited her and came back tut-tutting about how "the fool woman" was totally infatuated and wouldn't see reason.

Dulcie had cut her ties with her old life, married Giorgio Benetto, a Sicilian, and now lived in the shadow of Mount Etna. She had corresponded with Melanie, who had been secretly delighted with her aunt's unexpectedly adventurous spirit. Even the name of the estate, Terrafiore, had enthralled her, especially since she'd discovered that it meant *land of flowers*. She'd longed to be invited to visit and had even learned some Italian, in hope. But although Dulcie would have been glad to see her, she'd washed her hands of "your pigheaded father," and declined to invite him. Melanie's father's opinion of his sister was equally unflattering, and he'd refused to let Melanie fly to Sicily alone.

The years had passed. Melanie had gone to art college, and her life had become filled with new interests. She had a talent for making ceramics, and gradually she'd built up a clientele who valued her original designs. She began to market her product seriously, and before long she had a flourishing business. At last the invitation to Sicily had been repeated, only to be withdrawn when Giorgio had died unexpectedly.

Then had come news of Dulcie's own death, just one year after her husband's, and the incredible discovery that Terrafiore had been left to Melanie. She knew she couldn't possibly sell it without even seeing it, but she didn't try to explain all this to Harris, because he'd have thought she'd gotten windmills in her head. She knew he was irritated by her insistence on going to Sicily, because he'd almost persuaded her to marry him. Perhaps that was another reason for going. She felt pressured and needed a breathing space.

Marriage to Sir Harris Brennan would be a continuation of the life she'd always lived as Lady Melanie Carlyle, only daughter of Lord Carlyle. Apart from her business, it was a pleasant, tranquil existence, revolving around horses, dogs and English country pursuits, with servants always in the background and the deference she received as part of the local gentry. It was a life full of leisurely charm, but something had made Melanie delay giving Harris a final answer. She'd written to inform the Sicilian lawyer that she was coming to see her inheritance.

And now she was here, in an area that the guide book had warned her was the hottest place in all Italy, and she was beginning to wish she'd heeded the warning. The elegant linen pantsuit, which had seemed so suitable in England, was wilting in the furnace heat of Sicily. Already Melanie was longing to throw off her tights and trousers and go bare legged in a cotton skirt.

"Where's your sun hat?" Vittorio asked as he saw her fanning herself with a magazine.

"I don't have one."

"You must buy one in Catania," he said briefly.

"I wasn't sure if anyone would be meeting me," she said as they approached Catania. "Did my lawyer hire you? I mean—is this a taxi?"

He grinned, showing white teeth against his bronzed face. "No, a taxi would have been a little more comfortable. I'm part of Terrafiore."

"Oh, you mean you work for me?"

After a moment's hesitation he said, "I belong to the land."

The sudden air of dignity that fell over him made her almost shy of asking, "Have you—belonged to it very long?"

"All my life," he said simply.

From the airport to the port of Catania was barely five miles. To her surprise the town had a dead aspect, with shuttered shops and empty streets. "Siesta," Vittorio explained. "From twelve-thirty to four o'clock nobody moves. Luckily it's nearly time for them to open."

He stopped outside a door hung with a beaded curtain and showed her inside, where she found a trinket shop full of knickknacks. She lifted one of the straw hats that were hanging on the walls and was about to try it on when Vittorio gently but firmly removed it from her. "The signorina needs something much larger,'' he said to the assistant.

"Does she?" Melanie queried, slightly nettled by having him make her decisions.

"Naturally," he said, unruffled by her tone. "That's a tourist hat. We Sicilians choose something more sensible. This is better." He took a large floppy-brimmed hat from the assistant and fitted it onto her head, pulling it down firmly so that his brown fingers brushed her cheeks. Only a few inches separated them, and his vibrant masculinity struck her full force. It was an intensity that was concentrated in him, a vividness that made the lines of his body seem more sharply etched in the air than any other man's had ever been, an odor of spice and earth and primitive maleness that filled her nostrils and made her dizzy. Without warning, her heart had started to race.

He studied her with furrowed brow and nodded. "Don't wrap it up," he told the assistant. "The signorina will wear it."

He cocked an eyebrow, as if asking whether she was going to challenge him, but, as he'd said, the hat was perfect. The wide brim protected the nape of her neck and shaded her eyes, so Melanie swallowed her pique at his high-handedness, paid for the hat and returned to the car. Once out of the shop she managed to relax a little. The sensations that had invaded her a moment ago seemed absurd. Probably the heat was affecting her.

In a few minutes they were out of the city and driving through some of the most savagely beautiful countryside Melanie had ever seen. The colors were clear and piercing, seeming to rush at her. The land rose gradually before them, covered with orchards of oranges and lem-

ons, fenced in by low black walls covered in bougainvillea.

"The flowers seem to be growing directly out of the
stone," she said, puzzled.

"It isn't stone," Vittorio explained. "Those walls are
made of lava from Etna, which has covered this area
several times over the centuries. Lava is excellent for
growing things, so these parts are very fertile."

"What about Terrafiore?"

"The last time it was covered with lava was about eight
years ago. Its vineyards are still showing the benefit. Are
you feeling better?"

"Yes, thank heavens—it seems to be getting a little
cooler."

"That's because we're climbing."

"Is it far to Terrafiore?"

"About twenty miles."

The Jeep bumped over a stone in the road. She clung
on and turned slightly in her seat so that she could feel
more secure, and found herself looking at Vittorio. In the
hot, enclosed space she was sharply aware of the fact that
his flesh was barely covered. He had little body hair. His
shoulders were smooth and brown, as were his arms and
the calves of his legs.

Melanie knew that Sicily had often been invaded over
the centuries and that, as a result, Sicilians bore the
physical characteristics of many other races. When she
stole a glance at Vittorio's face, she saw that it had an
almost Greek beauty. His jaw was firm, his nose perfectly straight, with a finely chiseled appearance. Its
classical perfection made an intriguing contrast to the
curved, undisciplined contours of his generous mouth.
There was a hint of wildness about that mouth, a suggestion of dangerous unpredictability in the way the cor-

ners could smile or frown independently. The same spirit
was picked up in the tousled black hair, long enough to
brush the nape of his muscular neck and with a suggestion of curl.

In fact, she realized, everything about him was a study
in contrasts. He dressed like a peasant, but his speech was
educated. "Where did you learn such good English?" she
asked.

"In the beginning I learned in the school at Fazzoli.
You'll see Fazzoli soon. It's the nearest village to Terrafiore. Later I spent a year traveling, and visited England. I meant to stay away for longer, but I found I
couldn't. I *had* to come back to this land. Sicily doesn't
let you go."

She was about to ask him more when she heard a loud
tooting behind them. Turning, she saw a car a few yards
behind, driven by a middle-aged man with a red, ill-
tempered face, who was jabbing irritably on the horn.
Vittorio glanced in the mirror and cursed softly as he
slowed to a halt.

The car drew up beside them. It was flashily expensive
and looked incongruous in this wild terrain. The driver
matched the car perfectly, being also flashily expensive
and incongruous. He was heavily built, with jowls that
fell over the collar of his silk shirt. A silk handkerchief
was clutched in his pudgy hand and he used it constantly
to mop his sweating brow. As he heaved himself out and
approached Melanie with a shambling walk, he rear-
ranged his face into friendly lines.

"Signorina Carlyle?" he enquired, thrusting his hand
forward. "I am Pietro Salvani. No doubt you have heard
of me. I was hurrying to meet you at the airport. Alas, I
arrived too late. I shall never forgive myself that you had
to endure even a moment in this deplorable vehicle." The

last words were said with a sneer, and there was real dislike in the look he flashed at Vittorio, who returned it in full measure. Salvani spat something at him in Sicilian, and Vittorio retorted angrily in the same language. Melanie couldn't understand the words, but there was no mistaking the violent ill will between the two men.

Firmly she freed her hand, which Salvani had clutched in a damp grip. "It's very kind of you, Signor Salvani, but there was no reason for you to meet me."

"But of course I came to meet you. You're staying with my family while you're here."

This attempt to take her over wasn't at all to Melanie's taste, and she immediately responded, "Thank you, but I'd rather stay in my own place."

Salvani roared with laughter as if she'd made a huge joke. Beside her, Melanie could feel Vittorio's body stiff with hatred, and his mobile mouth was tense, as if he were biting back words with an almighty effort. "You must forgive me for laughing, *signorina,* but you're a stranger here. That dreary house out in the wilds, cut off from civilization, alone among a crowd of ignorant peasants—"

"My aunt found it very pleasant," she said firmly.

"But she lived there with her husband. You would be alone. I won't hear of you suffering such an ordeal. My wife is looking forward to caring for you. She won't forgive me if I return without you."

For a moment Melanie hesitated. She was used to her creature comforts, and the words "out in the wilds" and "cut off from civilization" made her uneasy. Perhaps she'd been foolish to rush out here after all.

"Let me take your bags," Salvani said.

"No," said Vittorio in a voice that made the other two stare at him. He ignored Salvani and spoke directly to Melanie. "Don't go with him. You *mustn't.*"

"Whatever do you mean?" she demanded, amazed at this presumption.

In his urgency Vittorio laid a hand on her arm. "I haven't time to explain, but you mustn't go with him. Please trust me, and do as I ask."

"What's this?" Salvani began to bluster. "Since when does a servant tell the *padrona* what to do?"

Melanie hardly heard him. Her eyes were held by Vittorio's. Despite his shabby clothes, he had a natural authority that prevented his demand from being outrageous. She could feel the pounding pulse in his wrist where he was holding her. Her own blood was racing, too, and it was suddenly impossible to do anything except what this man wanted.

"I think..." she said slowly, "that I'd better stay at Terrafiore, Signor Salvani."

"Nonsense, you don't know what you're saying. I'm getting your bags."

He went around to the trunk of the Jeep, but he'd scarcely touched it when Vittorio, moving at incredible speed, got between him and the vehicle and stood leaning on the trunk door. He didn't speak. He didn't need to. Every line in his body revealed a deadly threat.

Salvani shouted to Melanie. "Tell him to get out of my way."

"Let's not fight about it," she said. "It's best if I go to my own home."

Salvani stomped furiously back to the front window. "Don't you understand? This man is your servant, your paid hireling. Are you going to take orders from him?"

"I take orders from no man," she told him. "No man at all."

He understood the message in her frosty eyes and backed off, smiling to cover his defeat. "Of course—of course. I only wish to be your friend. My offer remains open for when you come to your—when you discover how unsuitable Terrafiore is for you. Good day, *signorina*." He took a glance at Vittorio's motionless figure watching him implacably, and hastily returned to his car.

Vittorio climbed into the driver's seat and looked at her. "You did the right thing," he said simply. "Thank you."

The idea of her employee thanking her for doing the right thing was so startling that it was a moment before Melanie could collect her scattered wits. As they drove on, she sat in brooding silence.

Melanie's mother had died when she was five, and she'd been reared by her father and one older brother, who'd adored her, indulged her and treated her much like a pet. She had enough self-awareness to know that she might easily have turned into a spoiled brat. That she hadn't was due partly to Dulcie's bracing common sense and partly to her own impish humor. But she still displayed the occasional imperiousness of one whose wishes had seldom been thwarted.

Salvani's efforts to dominate her had been doomed from the start, yet she'd found herself doing what Vittorio wanted quite naturally. It was unnerving to think about. But she hadn't actually been obeying Vittorio's commands, she reasoned, merely resisting Salvani's pressure. Yet the skin of her arm was still tingling where Vittorio had held it, and the memory of him saying urgently, "You *mustn't*" made the sudden color come to her cheeks. The blood raced in her veins as it had raced then.

When she was sure she could keep her voice steady, she asked, "What did he mean about you being my 'paid hireling'?"

"Just that. I'm your steward. My father was the steward before me. He taught me to love and care for Terrafiore."

"Why is Salvani so hostile to you?"

"Because I'm a good steward. Without me you'd have to sell to him or see the place go to rack and ruin. With me, you can tell him to go to hell." It was said without boastfulness or arrogance, simply as a plain statement of fact.

"What were the two of you shouting about?"

He shrugged. "It doesn't matter. You obviously got the feel of it."

"But I want to know," she insisted. When he didn't answer, she said crossly, "Vittorio, I mean it. You have to tell me."

"Why do I have to?"

"Because I'm your employer."

"My employer, not my owner," he said with a proud lift of his unruly head. "I belong to the land. Do you think *you* own the land? You're wrong. It owns you, just as it owns me. It won't let me go. That's why—" he broke off sharply.

"Yes," Melanie urged. "That's why..."

Instead of answering, he stopped the car and pointed into the distance. Following his direction, she saw a marvelous sight. A herd of wild horses came galloping down the hillside, manes and tails streaming out behind them. Melanie jumped eagerly from the car and stood watching, entranced by the beauty of the magnificent untamed creatures. She could feel the earth beneath her feet vibrating with their thunder, and the sensation thrilled her.

"What must it be like to ride one of them?" she breathed ecstatically.

"You can ride, then?"

"Of course," she said indignantly. "I was practically brought up on horseback."

The horses had ceased their headlong race and slowed to view the newcomers, cantering in circles, keeping a safe distance, tensed for sudden flight. Vittorio approached them gently and they skittered away, but after a moment they began to drift back. He made a soft high-pitched noise at the back of his throat, and immediately some of them wandered over and nuzzled him. He beckoned Melanie and she approached slowly, holding her breath. Vittorio was caressing the lovely creatures, murmuring words of love. Gradually, they crowded around him, accepting Melanie also. She stroked their noses and almost cried out with delight at their velvety softness.

Only one remained aloof. A stallion, magnificent in his gleaming blackness, kept a little distance apart, watching them warily. Vittorio called and the stallion took a few tentative steps forward before changing his mind and swerving sharply.

"Sometimes he lets me ride him," Vittorio said softly, "but the next time he'll lead me a dance and escape, leaving me thwarted, as though reminding me of how puny I am beside him."

He returned to the Jeep and came back with a rope halter that he'd taken from the back seat. He kicked off his sandals and began to stalk the stallion barefoot, the halter hidden behind him. The horse watched him, unblinking, until the last moment, when he reared up, turned sharply and streaked away, the sun shining on his glossy black coat. They watched him galloping into the distance. But then, just as suddenly, he turned and headed back to them, hooves pounding the earth like pistons. Again he veered away at the last minute, his eyes on Vittorio, who seemed to alarm and fascinate him at the same time.

This time, when Vittorio called, the stallion edged a little nearer and stood a few feet off, breathing hard. Man and horse held each other's gaze as the man crept closer, moving silently on bare feet. And then at last he slipped the makeshift halter on while the beast stood still. In a moment Vittorio was up on the broad back, and suddenly all docility disappeared. The horse reared and plunged, lashing out madly to dislodge his rider. A dozen times it looked as though Vittorio must be thrown, but somehow he clung on with feet and hands.

Then the stallion took off, racing away at top speed with Vittorio still on his back. Melanie stood, wonderstruck at his horsemanship as he circled and brought the animal back, then went off again in the other direction, man and beast fighting for control, but fighting as equals. The stallion cleared everything in its path, including a pile of rocks that would have smashed Vittorio to pieces if he'd fallen. But Melanie realized that it was no longer possible to tell where the horse ended and the man began. One brain seemed to control them both. And that brain was Vittorio's, achieving mastery not merely by power but by subtlety and empathy, reading the stallion's thoughts and anticipating him every time.

At last they came to a halt beside her, the stallion wearied to the point of docility, but unbroken all the same. His eyes still flashed, and instinct told Melanie that for Vittorio this was the only way. He would subdue horses, but not break their spirits, because he loved them, and her own love of them reached out to him with joy. She didn't even know that she was smiling as she looked up at him. She was aware of nothing but the way his damp clothes clung to him, revealing every line of his hard, athletic body, offering tantalizing hints of its power and grace. His chest was rising and falling slightly, and his eyes were bright from his battle.

"Do you want to ride with me?" he asked, and she nodded in dumb ecstasy.

He reached down and lifted her off the ground with one arm, swinging her up in front of him so that she settled astride the splendid black shoulders. She could feel the horse between her legs, not trembling but vibrating. Vittorio put his left arm firmly about her waist, drawing her back against him. With his free hand he held the halter, guiding and controlling the stallion.

Then the great muscles sheathed in black silk moved beneath her, and they were off again, galloping headlong to nowhere. She'd never ridden bareback before and was unprepared for the wonderful sense of unity with the horse, the awareness of every movement he made. There was still fire in him, but it was fire that had been brought under control by the man who sat behind her, his arm tight about her. She was sharply conscious of Vittorio's hand beneath her right breast, the fingers slightly splayed to give him a steady grip, the thumb almost touching her breast. The wind whipped past her face. She couldn't see where they were going. It didn't matter. She was transported to a new world where there was only thrilling physical sensation, and she wanted to gallop on forever.

She twisted to look up at Vittorio and saw that his unruly black hair was blown back from his face like the stallion's mane. He was smiling and his brilliant eyes seemed fixed on some far horizon, almost as if he'd forgotten her. But then he saw her looking at him, and suddenly he laughed out loud with exhilaration. She laughed wildly back. Her heart was thundering in a way she'd never known before. The pounding of the great hooves vibrated up through the stallion's body, through her thighs, her loins, making her gasp.

And then they were slowing. With dismay, she saw the Jeep come back into view and realized that it was over. As they came to a halt, she discovered that her blood was still galloping.

Vittorio jumped down first and stood looking up at her. "We are on Terrafiore," he said. "The stallion is yours if you wish to claim him. Shall I take him and break him in for you?"

She shook her head. "No. Let him go free."

He smiled. "I was sure you'd say the right thing." He put his hands about her waist and drew her forward. She held onto his shoulders, and for a moment she was dizzy with the certainty that he was going to kiss her. His generous mouth with the slightly parted lips seemed to loom very close. But instead he set her down and released her.

With the feel of solid ground beneath her feet, some of Melanie's common sense returned. Of course he wouldn't have kissed her. An employee would never think of it. But she knew an aching sensation that might almost have been disappointment.

Vittorio removed the halter and slapped the stallion's rump. Together they watched him gallop away. "I wonder if he'll ever come back to me," she said wistfully.

"But of course he will," Vittorio told her gently. "Because you let him go. He'll remember that."

His smile sent a tremor through her, and she realized that her common sense wasn't as certain as she'd hoped.

"I think," she said unsteadily, "that we should go on to the house now."

Two

As they drove on, the land changed abruptly, rising up in banks on either side of the road. The banks were covered in greenery, from which grew multitudes of flowers, red and white oleanders, jasmine, geraniums, and it was like moving through a tunnel of petals. Melanie turned her head a dozen times, trying to take in so much beauty.

Suddenly the road made an abrupt turn just up ahead, so that the bank seemed to cut across their path. On the top stood a young woman in her late teens. Melanie could see that she was unusually beautiful, tall and slender, with very long dark hair and olive skin. She was standing with her feet apart, her hands on her hips in a defiant stance, her eyes fixed on the approaching vehicle.

"That's Zenia," Vittorio said. "She works for you. Her mother is Annunciata, your housekeeper. They both speak English. They learned it from your aunt."

He thrust a hand up out of his window and waved to the girl. Melanie tried to see her better, but Zenia turned and ran springing over the ground like a young gazelle. "She's really lovely," she mused.

"Is she?" echoed Vittorio. "Yes, I suppose she is. I don't tend to notice because I've known her since she was in her cradle. I picked her up when she fell over, mended her dolls and thumped the other boys if they teased her. She's got a real spitfire temper, but you'll find she's a good maid. Dulcie said she knew how to look after clothes. She'll have gone back to tell the others you're here."

"We're near the house then?"

"You'll see it at any moment."

He turned the car just then and Melanie looked out. As the house came into view, she gripped the door, held silent by astonishment. Salvani's words had led her to imagine a small farmhouse of primitive design and shabby construction. But the magnificent villa that met her eyes was a two-story building, made of biscuit-colored stone with a red tile roof. Despite its size, the eucalyptus trees nestling close to it and the jasmine and clematis smothering the walls gave it a comfortable, homey appearance.

"You can only see part of it from here," Vittorio explained. "The building is actually oblong. That's one of the short walls. Inside, it's a figure eight, built around two square courtyards. Once there was a Roman villa here. Parts of it are still standing. The rest has been erected on the foundations."

"It's beautiful," she whispered.

Vittorio had slowed the Jeep for the approach. "Yes," he said quietly. "Yes, it is."

The wall was breached by a large wrought iron gate, which a man was pulling open. Several other people came out, until six men and women, including Zenia, were standing there watching their approach. Vittorio drove through the gate into a courtyard and stopped. "I have brought you the new *padrona,*" he said, loud enough to be heard by everyone.

He introduced her to the four men, who were all leathery and baked dark brown by the hot sun, and the two women. Zenia gave her an almost curt nod. Annunciata, her mother, was tall and thin, dressed in black. Her face could have been any age from forty to sixty, but her movements were strong and vigorous. She greeted Melanie with reserved courtesy. Like the others, she was watching her closely.

Melanie glanced around and saw that she was in a square courtyard with a fountain in the center. Cloisters lined two sides, their roofs supported by pillars covered in mosaics. Between the pillars stood fat tubs from which grew a riot of brilliantly colored geraniums. Vines spread over the other two walls—clematis, jasmine, bougainvillea. The whole atmosphere was one of peace, beauty and cheerfulness.

"I have a cool drink awaiting you inside," Annunciata said.

"That would be lovely," Melanie said.

"I'll take your bags up to your room," Vittorio told her.

Zenia said something in Sicilian that made her mother shake her head disapprovingly. "My daughter says she will go with Vittorio to make sure he doesn't make your room untidy," she explained to Melanie. "And it was a very rude thing to say," she added, with an eye on her daughter.

Vittorio grinned. "It's all right. She can say what she likes to her big brother."

A new brightness came to Zenia's eyes, and Melanie could tell she didn't like Vittorio speaking of himself as her brother. It was clear, too, that she'd seized on an excuse to go with him.

Annunciata led Melanie over the tiled floor of the cloisters and into the house, whose thick walls made it mercifully cool. The kitchen was full of delicious scents, and she understood why when she looked up and saw spices hanging from the rafters. Annunciata poured her a glass of cold white wine from an earthenware jug, and Melanie sipped it thankfully. There was bread, too, thick brown spicy bread, hot from the oven, sprinkled with olive oil.

"I must fetch more wine from the cellar," Annunciata declared and, lifting a wooden panel in the floor, she descended. Still eating her snack, Melanie went to stand at the window, passionately glad that she had come to this glorious, exotic place.

She heard voices above her head and peered out. Just above her, a pair of wooden shutters stood open, and through them she could hear Vittorio and Zenia, talking in pure Italian now, not Sicilian. Zenia sounded sulky. "Why do you reprove me for speaking our dialect, when we have always done so?" she was asking.

"I didn't reprove you," Vittorio replied soothingly. "I merely said it wasn't polite in front of someone who doesn't understand it."

"Oh, *her!* Why must everything be as *she* wants?"

Vittorio sighed, and Melanie thought she heard a touch of bitterness. "Because she is the *padrona*. Never forget that."

"Why do you take her part?" Zenia demanded passionately. "Why don't you hate her?"

Melanie tensed suddenly, listening for his reply. When it came, it was in a quiet voice that she had to strain to catch.

"Because I dare not," Vittorio answered somberly. "When a man allows himself to hate, there's no knowing what will come of it. Perhaps he may end by doing something that will make him hate himself."

Stunned, Melanie stood perfectly still, longing to hear more. Why should Vittorio hate her? What had brought that bitter, weary note to his voice? And what was he afraid of doing?

Annunciata returned from the cellar, bearing the full wine jug. "Terrafiore makes its own wine," she explained, "and it's stored down there in the earth, away from the heat. When you're rested I will show you. Now let me take you upstairs."

She led the way out into the spacious hall, where they found Vittorio and Zenia just coming down the stairs. "I didn't disarrange anything," Vittorio teased. He turned to Melanie. "With your permission, I will leave now. I suggest you have an early night to recover from your journey, and I will come first thing tomorrow to show you your property."

"Why don't you stay and eat with me?" she said. "Then you can tell me about Terrafiore."

He hesitated, almost uneasy. "It would be better if I didn't," he said at last, seeming to search for words. "I still have many duties to attend to. Until tomorrow."

He gave her a courteous little nod and departed, leaving Melanie feeling curiously snubbed. There was no hiding from it. He had made an excuse to avoid having dinner with her.

Her bedroom turned out to be enormous, with a huge old-fashioned double bed in the center. Melanie was used to the impressive proportions of Carlyle Hall, but even so, she felt swamped here. Annunciata explained that this had been Giorgio and Dulcie's room, and then Dulcie's alone.

"If you will give me the keys, I will do your unpacking," Zenia said coolly, when her mother had departed.

Melanie gave them to her and watched as Zenia dealt with her clothes. It took only a few moments to show that Dulcie had been right when she'd said Zenia was an excellent maid. The young woman handled the fine materials carefully but with confidence, and hung everything up in the proper way. Sometimes she paused to stroke a surface or admire a good cut, and Melanie realized how starved she must be for clothes that would do justice to her exotic beauty.

She began to look around, studying the tiled floor and huge walnut wardrobes. The room was relatively cool because the shutters over the windows had been closed against the heat of midday. There were four windows, two at each end of the long room. Melanie pushed one open and found a breathtaking view over the countryside. Terrafiore, in all its rich fertility, was spread before her, and just below it on the slope were the roofs of Fazzoli. She tried the other side, which overlooked the courtyard where she'd come in. Above it the mountain loomed, gently at first, then rearing up sharply toward the summit, where a pink glow illuminated the sky.

"That's Etna," Zenia said, following her gaze.

"You mean—you can't mean that it's erupting now?" Melanie asked uncertainly.

Zenia laughed, and Melanie had a feeling she was glad to have caught her out. "Of course not. But the flames never go out. The mountain is always on fire, deep in the earth, burning beneath our feet at this very moment.''

It was a disconcerting thought, but Melanie refused to let her face reveal her thoughts. Zenia's hostility was too blatant for that. ''How fascinating,'' she said.

Zenia shrugged and turned away to open a door. ''You have a bathroom through here. There is the shower.'' She demonstrated the taps.

''Where does the water come from?'' Melanie asked. ''We're so far out in the country.''

''We have our own well,'' Zenia explained. ''And our own generator for electricity.'' Her voice grew insolent. ''We also eat with knives and forks instead of using our fingers.''

Melanie flushed with anger. ''Don't ever speak to me like that again, or you'll leave.''

Zenia gave a hard laugh. ''If I leave my mother will leave, and the others will follow. You are nothing here without us. Why did you bother to come?''

''I came because Terrafiore is mine,'' Melanie said firmly.

A change came over Zenia's face, as though she would burst into tears. Then she turned and fled, leaving Melanie puzzled.

She spent fifteen minutes in the shower, and when she got out, the light, which had been just beginning to fade when she went in, had completely gone. She put on a cotton dress and went downstairs, commenting on the change to Annunciata.

''This is much farther south than in England,'' the housekeeper said, smiling. ''Darkness comes very suddenly. I have laid your evening meal in the dining room.''

Like everything else about the house, the dining table was huge. Melanie's place was laid in solitary state at one end. She dined royally off pasta and red peppers, followed by a deep-fried mixture of squid and shrimps, accompanied by Terrafiore's own white wine with its rare sulphurous taste from the volcanic earth. She finished with a cheese she'd never tasted before. She admired it enthusiastically and achieved her first success with Annunciata, who confessed to having made it herself with milk from the estate's cows. Melanie, who'd eaten in the most expensive and sophisticated restaurants in London, felt as if she'd supped with the gods at Terrafiore.

As she sipped her sweet black coffee, the weariness of the day suddenly hit her. Excitement had kept her alert, but now she longed for her bed. She rose to leave the table, and as she did so, a framed photograph on the mantelpiece caught her eye. She picked it up and saw that it was a man and a woman sitting close together, his arm about her shoulders. He was in his mid-fifties and still handsome in a burly way, with a fleshy face, sensual mouth and laughing eyes. The woman was also in mid-life but bore signs of having once been voluptuously good-looking, and her bathing dress revealed that she still had a good figure. A soft, blissful smile touched her mouth, as though she'd discovered a secret. Seeing how she nestled contentedly against the man, Melanie felt she knew what that secret was.

"That was Giorgio," Annunciata said as she began clearing the table.

"Who's the woman with him?" Melanie asked.

"Why, your Aunt Dulcie, of course."

Melanie laughed. "It can't be. Dulcie wasn't a bit like— good heavens, so it is!"

She looked more closely at the woman in the picture, astonished to realize that her dear straitlaced aunt had turned into this blissful hedonist whose whole body radiated physical fulfilment with the man holding her. Melanie had always seen her aunt's hair cut short and worn with severe bangs. Now the bangs were gone, the hair brushed back from the high forehead and grown in heavy waves to shoulder length. But the change in her went deeper than that. It had to do with the glowing sheen on her skin and the brilliance of her eyes. Now Melanie knew why Dulcie had never returned to England. In this rich, colorful place she had discovered passion and had remained, a happy prisoner in its spell.

And for no reason, the picture of Vittorio came into her mind, damp with sweat from the plunging of the horse, the heat of his trembling body communicating itself to hers. All the physical sensations of that moment rushed back to her with such violence that she grew dizzy and had to clutch the dresser for support.

Firmly she pulled herself together. It had been a long day and she was tired. A good night's sleep would make her see everything in proportion again. She started to replace the picture but stopped suddenly, alerted by something familiar in the man's face. She looked harder, trying to remember if Dulcie had ever sent her a photograph of Giorgio, but she couldn't recall it. Yet she was sure she'd seen him somewhere before.

At last she gave up, set the picture down and went upstairs. When she'd finished undressing she pushed open the shutters to look up the mountain to the summit, where the soft pink glow of the afternoon had been transmuted by the night into bloodred. Now she could see that it was a living light, dancing and shuddering against the darkness, apparently driven up from some furnace, fathoms deep in the earth. She watched, awed, until her eyes began to close. She slipped into bed, dropping into a deep sleep as soon as her head touched the pillow, but all that night her dreams were haunted by the sound of horses' hooves, and Vittorio's voice, saying that he was afraid to hate her because of what he might do.

She awoke to find blinding sunshine coming through the window whose shutters she'd left open. She jumped out of bed and looked out eagerly, finding everything as lovely as it had been the day before. The light had a different quality now, being the clear, cool radiance of dawn, but already she could feel the first suggestion of heat.

It was only seven o'clock, but the sounds coming from below told her that Annunciata was up and about. Melanie showered quickly and went downstairs, dressed for riding. She found Vittorio in the kitchen, munching a slice of bread and oil and drinking cold milk. "Are you ready to go?" he asked at once.

"Go where?"

"To see Terrafiore. We should start as soon as possible."

"I'd like some breakfast first, if you don't mind," she objected.

He immediately turned his fire on Annunciata. "Hurry up," he insisted. "Isn't it ready?"

"I can't start cooking until the *padrona* comes down," she protested indignantly. "Get out of my kitchen."

Vittorio laughed and took Melanie's arm. "I'll start showing you the buildings while you wait," he said, and before Melanie knew what was happening, she found herself swept out the door.

He took her through an arch in the wall that divided the two courtyards and she found that here there were no flowers growing and the atmosphere was functional. Two vehicles were parked in the yard; men came and went, always with a nod of respect to Vittorio.

"The place you've just left is the living quarters," he explained. "This part of the building is used for work. Up there are lofts for when the harvest is brought in. Now come and look here."

He led her into a long room that took up one side of the square. It was full of machinery, all standing silent. Melanie inspected a set of rollers, two giant stone wheels and some steel disks before exclaiming, "What on earth is it?"

"An olive press," Vittorio said. "The only one in this area. When the olive harvest starts in October your neighbors will bring their olives here to be turned into oil. You'll make a good profit from them, but an even bigger one from your own produce, because Terrafiore has the best olives in Sicily. Of course, some of it will go for the wages of the extra labor you'll hire, but you'll still do pretty well. You'll need to take on some men for the grain harvest, too, and that will start soon."

He showed her around the empty barns, explaining where everything went, until Annunciata came to summon Melanie to breakfast. She found two soft-boiled eggs on the table, done just as she liked them.

"Annunciata's good at producing an English breakfast," Vittorio explained. "That was what Dulcie always had." He left the kitchen, and Melanie sat down to her breakfast, which was delicious. Zenia hovered in the background, ready to attend to her, yet somehow making her uneasy. When Melanie's cup was empty, Zenia filled it at once, and superficially her behavior was perfect, yet there was a faint but perceptible air of defiance.

Vittorio reappeared. "I've told Leo to saddle Rosa for you," he said. "Leo's a kind of odd-job lad, and he has the ingenuity of the devil. When you're ready, we'll go out."

"I need to call England," Melanie said.

"You can do that from the post office in Fazzoli."

"Let's go then," Melanie said.

"Where's your sun hat?"

"Oh, I forgot. Zenia, would you get it for me? It's in my room."

Zenia departed without a word, and Melanie went out into the yard with Vittorio, where she found Leo waiting for her. He was a wiry little man who looked as if the fierce sun had shriveled him to a crisp. He grinned and indicated Rosa, a delicate bay mare that Melanie loved on sight. She wasn't like the magnificent black stallion, but she was gentle, with big, mild eyes. Zenia returned with the sun hat, which Vittorio took from her and settled onto Melanie's head, pulling it down firmly as he had before. Again she had the shocking, sweet-sharp sensation that the nearness of this man could give her. She drew in her breath, smiling to cover her sudden disturbance, and in the same moment her eyes met Zenia's. The girl was regarding her with undisguised hostility. Of course, Melanie thought, Zenia was infatuated with Vittorio and had sensed Melanie's reaction to him. The next moment Zenia had turned away and flounced into the house.

They mounted and Vittorio led the way under the arch into the outside world. As the horses walked, he indicated the land ahead of them, which fell away slightly. "This is all Terrafiore, and behind you, where it climbs out of sight. Down there are your orchards. Let's see them first."

They cantered on, and he led her through a bewildering array of fruit trees, oranges, lemons, rich, luscious peaches hanging from the branches. Vittorio cut some peaches and put them into a bag attached to his saddle. "We'll have them for lunch," he said.

Before Melanie could catch her breath, they were riding through the vineyards, which seemed to stretch for miles. "I can't believe this," she murmured. "I thought Terrafiore was a little farm."

"It's the best estate in Sicily," Vittorio said with simple pride. "That's why Salvani wants it. He's ruined his own land through greed and stupidity, so now he thinks he'll take over a well-run place and reap the rewards. Only he wouldn't. He'd ruin Terrafiore, too, if he got his hands on it. He's the sort of man who'd expect his olives to give him a good harvest every year."

"Now you make me feel ignorant," Melanie said. "Why shouldn't they give a good harvest every year?"

"The olive's a temperamental plant. It gives its best every three years." Vittorio explained seriously. "For the other two, it takes a rest. It's the way of olives. You have to plan for it by planting them in rotation and leaving them to get on with it. But Salvani won't accept that. He sprays them with everything on the market, uses every newfangled fertilizer that comes out, whether it's suitable for volcanic soil or not—and few of them are—and then wonders why his plants wilt. He wants to make money quickly, but you can't rush nature.

He looked at her with sudden intensity. "You mustn't sell to Salvani. Terrafiore needs love and careful cultivation. He'll squeeze every last penny out of it and leave it barren. *It must not happen.*"

For a moment she was on the verge of promising to do whatever Vittorio said. His eyes held hers with hypnotic intensity, compelling her. She could feel her heart beginning to beat quickly, and for some reason it alarmed her.

She was in a strange land. She needed to keep her wits sharp. But Vittorio seemed able to shake her control too easily. She took a deep breath and recovered her poise. "Why don't we go and find that telephone?" she asked.

He sighed, as if recognizing that he'd pushed too hard and made an error. "Certainly," he said. "I'll take you to Fazzoli."

Fazzoli turned out to be a village of about fifteen thousand people, built on a gentle slope. It was connected to Catania by a bus that ran three times a day, had one good hotel, two small *pensiones*, and one main post office. But there were several dozen sweet shops and tobacconists where, as in the rest of Italy, stamps and bus tickets were also for sale. And on every corner was a small establishment declaring itself a "bar," but which, in addition to alcohol, sold soft drinks, cakes and ice cream.

From the curious looks that greeted her as she entered the post office, Melanie guessed that news of her arrival had already gone around the locality. She gave Harris's number in England, and after a few minutes she was put through.

"At last," she heard his voice. "Darling, why didn't you call me yesterday, as soon as you reached the house?"

"There's no phone there. I'm calling from the village."

"No phone! Good grief, what sort of primitive place is it?"

"It's not primitive. It's actually rather beautiful, but it's a bit far out in the country."

"You mean you're stuck out in the wilds?"

"Well—it *is* wild, but it's a magnificent sort of wildness, if you know what I mean." As she said the words, she realized that Harris wouldn't know at all. The soft, rolling hills of England were wild enough for him.

"Have you seen Salvani yet?"

"Yes, he wanted me to stay with his family—"

"But darling, that would be ideal. Why didn't you?"

"I don't know. I just felt he was being pushy. It might be awkward being in his house if I'm not going to sell."

"Not going to— what madness is this? What else can you do but sell?"

"I don't know. Perhaps while I'm here, I'll find out. Look, I just rang to let you know I'm all right. I'll call again soon."

She hung up and stood staring at the phone, trying to understand an unnerving thing that had just happened to her. She was almost sure that she loved Harris. She would probably marry him. Yet she suddenly had trouble remembering what he looked like.

Nonsense! It was just that in this vivid country she was besieged with new impressions, and they had temporarily blurred the old ones. Vittorio, for instance, was an oddity, a man who had caught her attention because she was so much in his hands. There could be no comparison with Harris, who was the solid reality in her life.

Her next task was to call on Dr. Bartolli, the lawyer, prove her identity and sign the papers that made her the legal owner of Terrafiore. He was an austere, elderly man who seemed slightly bemused at her presence here. When she told him she intended to stay awhile, he frowned and made a short speech about the advantages of selling quickly, but when she stood her ground, he said he would notify the bank, open an account for her and have the estate's funds put in her name. Melanie found his demeanor depressing and was glad to escape back into the sun. Vittorio was waiting for her, a bottle of wine in his hand. "I bought it for our lunch," he said. "I'll show you the upper slopes and we'll eat there."

They rode on through orchards of banana, fig and eucalyptus trees, through olive groves and more vineyards. Between the orchards, flowers lined the roads, their brilliantly colored petals held up to the sun. Wherever she looked, Melanie saw the same picture of rich fertility and glorious abundance. She tried to think of the English countryside, which had always seemed perfect to her before, but it was pale in her mind, its pastel colors unable to compete with the splendid, life-affirming vividness all around her. And Harris? She'd brought his face back to mind now, but didn't he, too, seem a little pallid? She pulled herself back from the thought, feeling guilty at her disloyalty.

At last, the cultivated land fell away behind them and they were in wild countryside. Vittorio led her to a place where there were trees and a small stream that ran rapidly downhill. The water was pleasantly and unexpectedly cold. They sat on the grass, and Vittorio put the wine bottle into the water, wedged between two small rocks. He peeled the peaches with a knife taken from his belt. When he'd finished, he handed one to her and she tasted it.

"Oh, it's good," she said blissfully. "I've never tasted a peach like it before."

"Of course," he said, mock indignant. "That's a Terrafiore peach, a *real* Sicilian peach, not the cotton wool you get in other countries. But don't insult God's good fruit by nibbling it as though you were afraid. Bite right into it."

He demonstrated with his own peach, and the rich juice spurted out. Melanie laughed and did the same, feeling the juice running down her chin and over her fin-

gers, so that she gasped and scrabbled for a handkerchief.

Vittorio laughed. "That's how the good things of life
should be enjoyed," he advised, "with joy and gratitude." He sank his white teeth into the luscious fruit
again, and Melanie was suddenly reminded of pictures
she'd seen of pagan deities. At this moment, Vittorio
might have been Pan, lusty, earthy, redolent of life. He
smiled at her, and the curving sensuality of his lips
seemed like a promise and a challenge.

He leaned down into the stream to wash off the juice,
and came up sputtering, shaking brilliant drops of water
into the air, where they caught the sun. She couldn't help
laughing at him. "I looked out of my window last night,
and the sky seemed to be on fire," she told him.

He nodded. "Etna's a fine sight."

"I hadn't realized that went on all the time. I thought
volcanos lay quiet between eruptions."

Vittorio laid his hand on the ground. "Listen."

She leaned down, and from deep in the earth's belly
she heard a continuous grumbling roar, so soft that she
had to strain to be sure it was there.

"Etna never sleeps," Vittorio said. "Once you've
heard her murmuring, you'll never be completely un-
aware of it again. Nothing's going to happen just now,
but she likes to remind us not to forget that she's there,
and that it's only by her favor that we live here. Her last
eruption was only eight years ago. It streamed right over
where we are now."

"It seems strange that something dangerous should
cause the earth to flower so beautifully."

"There's nothing strange in danger and beauty going
hand in hand," he said. "Sometimes they can't be separated."

She felt the ground on which she was lying and sensed it again, a soft, thunderous thrumming, like a giant heartbeat, vibrating up through her whole body, reminding her of nature's ruthless bargain, on which Terrafiore's prosperity was built. She'd come to a land of savage contrasts and brutal beauty, a land in which the total absence of clouds made the sky seem higher, and the clearness of the air gave the colors a brilliance that almost hurt her eyes.

Then she saw Vittorio's eyes on her, and she knew he'd meant more than his words had seemed to say. She wondered if she was letting her imagination run riot. There was something about him at that moment that made her sharply aware of both beauty and danger.

"Salvani will be pressing for his answer soon," Vittorio reminded her. "Don't you see now that you mustn't sell to him?"

"But if I keep Terrafiore, I'll have to stay in Sicily."

"Then stay," he said at once. "Why not?"

She could have said she must return to England because of the man who was expecting her to marry him, but for some reason she didn't. Instead she prevaricated, "I have a life in my own country. I can't just toss it aside overnight."

"Dulcie did. She was happy here."

By accident or design, he'd said exactly the right thing. "I wish I'd seen Dulcie in this place," Melanie said. "How did she seem to you?"

"Like a flower that had waited a long time to open."

"You sensed that, too?" she said eagerly. "I saw her picture last night, and she seemed so different from what I remembered."

"You mean she didn't look English anymore?" he asked with a hint of mockery. "She became a Sicilian. She discovered that she had roots in the earth."

"Well, we know about that in England, too," she protested, slightly nettled. "All my family grew up in the country."

"Ah, yes, on the great estate, the lordly acres, owned by a gentleman farmer with a title. That's not the same. I'm talking about *earth* that you know personally, intimately, that you love and hate and fight until it yields up its fruits—earth that you have to protect from drought and tremors and lava, that will break your heart and your back but repay you a thousand times over. It doesn't belong to you until you've put your hands deep into it and got them dirty."

Suddenly he thrust his hands into the ground near the stream, where it was damp, seized a handful and held it up. Something in his eyes compelled Melanie to take it and inhale its rich odor. "There is life and death in the earth," Vittorio said, "blood and anguish, pain and sweat. But above all, there is love. Only when you love it will it truly belong to you."

She looked up at him, startled by the intensity in his voice. A man praying to a terrible deity might have used that tone of possession and anger and passionate dedication. She had the feeling that Vittorio had bared his innermost soul to her, that nothing went deeper with him than this love of the earth, that he was inviting her, pleading with her to share with him. Suddenly the light answer with which she'd intended to put him off refused to come to her lips. "I don't know...." she said uneasily. "It's too much to decide all at once—"

"Then don't decide. Make Salvani wait. But don't sell to him until you've learned to know *this*." He closed his hands over hers so that the soil was trapped between them. He had large, shapely hands. They were warm and hard, and through them she could feel the barely leashed power of his body. His whole being vibrated with intensity, and again she had the disturbing sensation that they were discussing something sacred.

When she still hesitated, he said earnestly, "Listen, I'll tell you what I wouldn't tell you yesterday—what Salvani shouted at me. He said I'd known that he was planning to collect you from the airport, and he accused me of hurrying to reach you first. It's true. I had to get you out of his clutches while there was time. Once he had you, you'd have signed over Terrafiore without knowing what you were doing."

"You have a very poor opinion of me," she said with a touch of indignation. She released her hands, feeling as though she were breaking the hypnotic spell he was weaving about her. "I'm not so spiritless. Salvani doesn't worry me. I've coped with difficult men before." She saw his wry grin and demanded, "What's so funny?"

"Just that you might not cope with him so well if I weren't here. Luckily I am."

His self-assurance nettled her, and she said coolly, "That would be all very well if I needed a protector, but I don't. I may not be a Sicilian, but I'm not a half-wit. Now I suggest we go back."

"Not yet. I still want you to—"

"And *I* want to go back," she said firmly. She'd had enough of taking Vittorio's orders. "You've done your job in showing me around my property, and now I'd like to make up my own mind."

She sensed rather than felt him flinch. His lips tightened, but he got to his feet in silence. When he'd retrieved the horses, his expression was blank, but an air of reserve had settled over him.

"If the *padrona* is ready," he said formally, "I will take her home."

Three

——

The first thing they saw when they arrived home was Salvani's ostentatious car, which made Vittorio's mouth twist into an expression of contempt. Salvani himself emerged from the house and threw up his arms in greeting. "*Signorina,* I gave myself the pleasure of calling on you earlier, but I just missed you."

"I went into Fazzoli," she said, jumping down.

"I wish I'd known. I'd have sent my car for you."

"The *padrona* prefers riding," Vittorio said with a jeering grin. "You should try it, Salvani."

The older man's eyes narrowed, and pure malice gleamed from them as he spat something in Sicilian. Vittorio laughed.

"Perhaps I could have a few words with you *alone,*" Salvani said significantly to Melanie.

"Of course, let's go inside. Please put the horses away, Vittorio."

He took her bridle and gave her an ironic little bow. The sarcastic humor had vanished from his face, and he was smoldering with anger.

"I'm glad to see you've started putting that one in his place," Salvani observed as they went indoors.

Melanie refused to answer this. She was slightly ashamed of the spurt of temper that had made her pull rank on Vittorio. She'd felt pressured and overpowered by him and sought refuge in an imperious manner that came easily to her. She made a silent resolution to be more careful in future. "Has Annunciata given you any refreshment?" she asked Salvani.

"Some chilled wine and fruit from your own orchards."

"I hadn't realized Terrafiore was so bountiful. I'd pictured it as just a little farm, but I think it must be one of the most beautiful places I've ever seen."

Salvani frowned. "But you should beware," he said. "You're a northerner, and they never do well in this climate."

"I've already caught a touch of the sun," she admitted, rubbing her arms. "I must be more careful in future."

"You sound as though you plan to stay here?" he asked slowly.

"I think I will, for a while. I've only just discovered Sicily. I don't want to lose it again so soon. Did you have something particular you wished to say to me?"

"Yes, I came to invite you to dinner at my house. All my family are eager to meet you."

"I'd like that."

"How about tonight?"

"I'll look forward to it."

"My car will be here for you at seven o'clock. I'll leave now, and go to tell my wife the good news."

He took up his hat and gusted out like a linen-clad elephant. Melanie followed him into the courtyard and watched as he squeezed himself behind the wheel and drove away. As she had half expected, Vittorio appeared at once. "I suppose you were listening," she said, exasperated.

"I held myself in readiness in case you needed me. You don't know Salvani. I do."

"Why was he so annoyed when you talked about riding?"

"Because he's a coward. He hasn't been up on a horse since he was thrown."

"So of course you had to taunt him?"

"It doesn't do any harm to remind such a man that he's a worm," Vittorio said coolly. "You should remember it, too, and avoid him, not dine with him."

Despite her good resolution, his autocratic manner goaded her again. She took a deep breath. "Thank you for your advice, Vittorio, but if you don't mind, I'll decide my own relationship with my neighbors."

She turned and was about to head for the house when she was stopped by Vittorio's grasp on her arm. The sudden feel of the warm hand against her skin made her gasp, and she raised her gaze to meet his. There was a strange sparkling light in his eyes as he viewed her. "You forgot to give the servant his dismissal," he said softly.

"How dare you! Release me at once!"

"Do I have the *padrona's* leave to go?"

"*Yes.*" She shook herself free and ran inside, uncomfortably aware that the blood was pounding through her body. She went up to her room, longing to be cool again. Zenia had already closed the shutters against the fierce noon heat. Looking through the crack, Melanie could see Vittorio below, giving orders to some workmen in the yard. She'd been here only twenty-four hours, and that short space of time had been filled with this man, who seemed to have the power of blotting out everything else.

But her independent spirit resisted. She had no intention of letting Vittorio dominate her. He might simply be concerned about the land, but instinct warned her that there was another element to the situation that she hadn't discovered. He was more dangerous than Salvani because he left her with fewer defenses. She remembered yesterday, when they had ridden the horse together, their bodies perfectly attuned. The thought that he might kiss her had burned into her consciousness so deeply that even now the memory made her blush. If she was honest with herself, she knew she'd wanted that kiss from a man she'd known only a couple of hours, wanted it with a burning need that had never troubled her with Harris.

At that moment Vittorio looked up from the yard, straight at her window. She stepped quickly back into the shadows, hoping he couldn't have seen her standing at the crack, watching him. Her pride rose, combatting the strange sensations that were coursing through her. Vittorio was too sure of himself where she was concerned. She'd done well to take her own line about Salvani.

She was waiting downstairs when the car arrived that evening. To her relief the air was cooler, and the white silk chiffon dress she wore with the little matching jacket and silver sandals, was ideally suited to the evening. The chauffeur held the rear door open for her and she got in. She'd half expected Vittorio to hover disapprovingly over her departure, but there was no sign of him.

It was ten miles to Salvani's house. Melanie pulled down the window and looked out, trying to take in the scenery, but the light faded too quickly for her to see very much. Once though, when the car slowed for a turn, she had an odd impression of hearing hoofbeats far off in the darkness. But when she listened carefully she heard nothing, and she decided she was imagining things.

Salvani's house, on the outskirts of Fazzoli, was floodlit, which enabled Melanie to see that, like his car, it was modern and ostentatious. Clearly money had been lavished on it, yet it lacked the mystery and elegance of Melanie's villa. Her host and his wife, Irena, were waiting on the step to greet her. Irena was a tall, masterful-looking woman with broad shoulders and a stubborn jaw. She embraced Melanie, kissing her once on each cheek, then took her arm firmly, as if making sure she didn't escape.

The Salvani family consisted of one son and five daughters, who were uncannily alike, each having inherited their mother's grim good looks and their father's cold eyes. All the daughters were married and here tonight with their husbands. Salvani introduced his sons-in-law, mentioning that this one was a banker, that one a local politician, as though their status was all he knew about them. Melanie uttered a formal politeness about how proud he must be of his distinguished family, and he responded as if she'd congratulated him on a successful coup. "It's a great responsibility being the father of daughters," he said. "But I fancy I've done the best for them."

Like their wives, the sons-in-law mostly came out of the same mold, being haughty, fleshy and dull looking. The only exception was Franco, who was married to Virgilia, the middle daughter. He was in his mid-twenties, several years younger than his wife, and seemed awkward among his overpowering in-laws. Salvani introduced Franco briefly and didn't mention his occupation, the only time he omitted to do this. Melanie smiled at the young man, liking him for his shyness, so noticeable in this confident company, and he smiled nervously back before shooting an anxious look at his wife.

The dinner was served at a long oak table, lit with candles, decorated with flowers and leaves. Efficient servants glided silently in and out, plying Melanie with some of the most delicious food she had ever tasted. Everything was new to her, starting with the pasta *con sarde,* a concoction of pasta with fresh sardines, anchovies, pimento, raisins and saffron. She washed it down with Fuoco dell'Etna, a robust red wine, one of the many produced locally.

Then followed swordfish steak, grilled and served with lemons, capers and herbs. For this the wine was Etna Bianco, a delicious golden liquid with a rare taste that Irena told her came from the volcanic soil. "You should have accepted our invitation to stay with us," Irena said, smiling with satisfaction at Melanie's appreciation.

"Unluckily, I arrived too late to save her from that oaf, Farnese," said Salvani with a sigh.

"Then you'll be to blame for any misfortune that befalls our guest," his wife reproved him. "How can she be expected to know what a bad lot he is?"

"He doesn't seem like a bad lot to me," Melanie observed in a mild voice that hid her sudden inner tension.

"Oh, he knows how to seem pleasant," Irena agreed. "But he's a greedy, unscrupulous, calculating wretch, who has his sights fixed on one thing, and one thing only. You should never forget that in your dealings with him."

"And what is this one thing?" Melanie inquired.

"Seizing Terrafiore, of course," Irena said. She saw Melanie looking at her with a puzzled frown. "Has nobody told you?"

"Told me what?"

"That Vittorio Farnese is Giorgio's son."

Melanie stared. "Giorgio? You mean the man Dulcie married?"

Irena nodded. "I'm afraid so. Of course it's all supposed to be a secret. Officially he's the son of Enrico Farnese, the steward, but everyone knows Giorgio chased after Enrico's wife. He never acknowledged Vittorio, even after both the Farneses were dead, but he paid to send him abroad, and everyone thought he'd leave Terrafiore to him. But he didn't."

"Then perhaps Vittorio isn't Giorgio's son, after all," Franco ventured to say.

Salvani regarded him with weary distaste. "Did anyone ask you?"

"Well, no—but—"

"Then shut up."

Franco subsided. Melanie sat in silence, trying to come to terms with the incredible thing she'd just learned. Now she knew why Giorgio's face had struck her as familiar. There was a slight but perceptible resemblance to Vittorio. It was true. Vittorio was Giorgio's son and he had a claim on Terrafiore. This was why Zenia had expected him to hate her.

"I don't suppose Vittorio happened to mention this to you, did he?" Salvani asked.

"No, he never said anything," she said quietly.

"I'd lay money that he's been playing the role of the devoted steward," Salvani jeered. "But don't be deceived. He's laying his plans in the dark. He's a bad lot. For years he's considered himself the heir, and now he won't be scrupulous about what he has to do to recover his 'rights.' Why do you think he's still working there? He's as proud as the devil. How could a proud man bear to work on land that he thinks should be his—unless he's hoping to get hold of it?''

Melanie didn't answer. The seed Salvani had planted had taken root and pushed up shoots of suspicion. In the short time she'd known Vittorio she'd felt a sense of almost devastating closeness to him. But it had been based on quicksand. He knew something she didn't, was thinking thoughts she hadn't dreamed of. Perhaps he was making plans that must be concealed from her. Suddenly the way he'd hurried to the airport to reach her before Salvani, seemed ominous.

To cover her dismay, she smiled and said with a rather forced laugh, ''Well, anyway, now that Terrafiore is mine, there's nothing he can do.''

''He can charm you out of it,'' Salvani said at once. He patted her hand. ''You will forgive me for mentioning that it's known that English ladies are—shall we say—susceptible to Latin charm.''

''I'm not in the least susceptible to it,'' she said, removing her hand and looking him steadily in the eye. As she'd guessed, he didn't understand the hint, but his shrewd-eyed wife stirred uneasily.

''He'll tell you pretty stories to make your head spin,'' Salvani predicted. ''He may even pretend that he loves you, but it's all for one reason—to steal from you. You'll be better off selling to me before he does you any harm.''

''He didn't do any harm to Dulcie,'' Melanie observed. ''He seems to have run the estate pretty well for her.''

"Dulcie was Giorgio's wife," Irena said. "Naturally she inherited. Even he would respect that. It's now that the danger comes."

"We'll see," Melanie said noncommittally. "I must tell you that I haven't made up my mind about selling yet."

"But there's nothing else you can do," Salvani expostulated.

"I could stay and run Terrafiore. Dulcie did."

"Dulcie was dependent on Vittorio Farnese," Salvani growled. "I've already explained to you the danger of *you* being dependent on him, and I'd have thought it was obvious—"

He stopped abruptly because his wife had thrown him a warning look. Melanie had a feeling of watching a well-drilled team in which Irena was the brains and her husband the brawn. To her relief, Irena was astute enough to let the subject drop.

The final courses appeared, puff pastry filled with honey, sugar and sesame seeds, accompanied by Marsala and followed by strong black coffee. The rest of the time passed so pleasantly that Melanie could almost believe she'd imagined the tension at the dinner table. The only jarring note was poor Franco, who seemed to be regarded as negligible by the entire family, not least his wife, although she was weighed down by jewelry, which, as she never tired of telling everyone, had been lavished on her by her devoted husband.

At last the evening was over. Salvani escorted Melanie down the steps to his waiting car, showed her into the front passenger seat and settled himself into the driver's seat. "I escort our honored guest home myself," he declared.

In a moment they'd left his palatial driveway and were gliding through Fazzoli. Then the little town was behind them and they were out in the wild countryside. The headlights lit up the stony road ahead, but when Melanie pressed her face to the window, she couldn't see another light for miles.

"Do you know where we are?" Salvani inquired.

"No, but I suppose we can't be far from Terrafiore," she said.

Salvani laughed. "Near or far. What difference does it make when you don't know the way?"

"Then it's fortunate I have you to drive me home," she said politely.

"Yes, isn't it?" he agreed, and at that very moment the car came to a sudden stop.

"What's the matter?" Melanie asked.

"I thought we could talk more comfortably here," Salvani said, turning in his seat to face her and blasting her with the smell of garlic.

"We have nothing to talk about," Melanie said firmly, "and I'd like to go straight home."

"Now wait, wait, don't be so impatient. We haven't yet discussed the sale. I've offered you a fair price and I've put up with your shilly-shallying, but now my patience has run out."

"And so has mine," Melanie said firmly, "Please take me home at once."

For an answer Salvani merely grinned. And suddenly Melanie realized how very much she was in his power in this lonely spot with not a light to be seen in any direction. "Take me home," she said, more firmly than she felt.

"But of course—just as soon as we've settled the sale," Salvani said.

"You're crazy if you think this is the way to persuade me."

"I'm afraid it's the *only* way to persuade you, because I can see you're prepared to be difficult. Dulcie was difficult, too. I spent a lot of time working on her, and I'd very nearly succeeded when the silly woman died. I don't have any more time to waste, so I'm forced to adopt more direct methods with you."

She controlled her rising temper and said with deadly calm, "What do you hope to gain by this? Even if I agreed to sell, I'd take it back the minute I left you. Haven't you thought of that?" she added sarcastically.

"But of course. That's why I had the document prepared. Here." He reached into the glove compartment and pulled out a paper that he gave to her. "You'll see that the witnesses have already signed. Only your signature is missing."

"Go to hell!" she told him flatly.

Salvani sighed as if wondering how anyone could be so stupid, leaned back in his seat and tilted his hat over his eyes, in the manner of a man prepared to wait out the night. Furiously Melanie cursed herself for being so foolish as to get into this situation. She underestimated her danger. Now that Salvani had shown his hand, he *had* to get her signature tonight, or he'd lost.

But Salvani had underestimated *her*. There was no way she was giving in to blackmail. She took up the paper and made a pretense of looking it over, though she had no intention of signing it.

"It's all perfectly fair," Salvani said. He was watching her like a snake from beneath the brim of his hat.

"I'll see it better with my reading glasses," she said, and delved into her evening bag.

"Now you're being sensible," he said.

Suddenly she made a quick turn toward the door. Salvani lunged to forestall her, slamming his hand down over the handle, but the next minute he'd jerked back, howling with pain, the back of his hand streaming with blood from two wounds that Melanie had inflicted with her nail scissors, "You bitch!" he raged, and choked off into silence as he found the two wicked little points being held an inch away from his eyes.

"I'll do anything you force me to," she said deliberately.

She reached behind her and managed to undo the handle, then backed out of the car, not taking her eyes off him. She slammed the door and began to run.

He came after her at once. She eluded him for a while, but the bumpy road surface made it hard to run in her delicate shoes, and at last he caught up. He was twice her size and brutally strong. Melanie defended herself madly, but the scissors were less effective out in the open, and although she cut him a few times, he soon began to overpower her. With despair she felt herself being dragged helplessly back to the car. She tried to scream, but struggling had left her short of breath.

He reached the car and held her there with one huge paw clasped around her wrist while he fumbled with the handle. She tried to bite his hand, but he held it easily out of danger, laughing at her efforts, a nasty, sinister sound that made her blood run cold.

And then suddenly she heard another sound, one that filled her with wild hope, if only it wasn't a hallucination. Salvani must have heard it, too, for he stopped a moment, listening. There it was, louder this time, the blessed sound of hoofbeats galloping, getting near. Salvani uttered an oath and tried to drag her into the car, but the next moment a huge horse appeared in the glare of the headlights. Melanie caught a brief glimpse of Vittorio's face, blazing with hate as he launched himself from the horse's back, straight for Salvani's throat.

Both men landed on the ground, but Vittorio sprang to his feet again at once, hauling Salvani up by his tie and delivering one hammer punch. Salvani's legs gave way. He slithered down the car and sat there, staring stupidly up at them, still conscious but apparently unable to move.

"Come along," Vittorio said. He leaped onto the animal's back and reached down for her. Melanie felt herself drawn up easily by powerful arms and settled sideways in front of him. He gave a faint click and the horse moved off.

She was trembling with shock. To stop herself from falling, she put her arms around Vittorio, taking comfort from the strong, warm column of his body. "Thank God, you were there," she whispered.

"I was never far away from you," he said, slipping one arm about her waist to steady her. "I knew Salvani would try some beastliness, so I stayed nearby."

"You were near me—all the time?" she asked in wonder.

"I followed the car to his house, at a discreet distance, and waited outside until you emerged. As soon as I saw he meant to drive you home himself I knew there was going to be trouble. I blame myself for letting the car get so far ahead of me. I should have been there sooner."

She was moved by the thought of him waiting patiently outside for her all evening. She raised her eyes to look at him. "You tried to warn me," she said. "I should have listened."

"Never mind that now. The important point is that you're safe."

In the darkness she could just make out the way he smiled reassuringly down at her. "What did you do to make him yell?" he asked.

"Stabbed him with my nail scissors."

He gave a shout of laughter that echoed around the hills. "Good for you. Under that demure exterior you have the spirit of a Sicilian." He felt her trembling against him and tightened the arm about her waist. "What is it?"

"Reaction, I guess. If you hadn't been there—"

"But I was there," he said, "as you should have known I would be."

And it suddenly seemed very natural and inevitable that he should have been watching over her. Melanie relaxed, holding on to him firmly with both arms, surrendering to the rhythm of the horse.

Near the gate to Terrafiore, he stopped. "I'll set you down here," he said.

"Aren't you coming in?"

"No."

She began to slide down, but at the last moment Vittorio's arm tightened, his immense strength holding her off the ground as if she weighed nothing. She looked up and something caught in her throat at the sight of his face so close to hers. Then he pulled her against him and crushed her mouth with his own.

For a moment, shock held her rigid. Then everything else melted away before the delight of feeling his lips against hers, kissing her hard. There was no tenderness. She could feel how hard was his body, and he kissed her as though he were fighting her—or himself. But the physical tension between them, which she'd sensed ever since the first moment of meeting him, had suddenly culminated in this moment of fierce passion, and she responded helplessly. She reached out her free hand, meaning to slide it behind his head, caressing him.

But in the same moment she felt him lowering her to the ground. She made a sound of protest, but he was drawing apart from her. She could hear his breath coming raggedly and see his eyes burning like coals in the darkness, but he was master of himself. He set his jaw grimly, as though determined to let this go no further. Melanie felt the ground beneath her feet and could have cried out at the beauty that had been snatched away so soon.

"Go inside," he said.

"Vittorio—"

"No," he cried hoarsely, *"leave me."*

Before she could protest further, he'd wheeled his horse and galloped away. Melanie stood, staring into the darkness, feeling an aching sense of deprivation.

She heard the gate being opened behind her. The sound of their arrival had roused the house. Leo let her in, and Annunciata came out into the courtyard to greet her. "Didn't Salvani bring you home?" she asked, looking around for the car.

"Let me get inside and I'll tell you about Salvani," Melanie said bitterly.

Over coffee in the kitchen, she described everything that had happened. Annunciata made shocked noises, but Zenia listened with a kind of angry delight. "Was Franco there?" she asked with a gleam in her eye.

"Yes, do you know him?"

"I used to. Of course he doesn't recognize his old friends since he married into a fine family," Zenia added sourly.

"He didn't look as if it had made him very happy. He seemed like a frightened rabbit." Melanie described how the family treated Franco, and Zenia threw back her head and crowed with laughter.

"Serve him right," she said at last. "Oh, I'm so glad to know that."

Annunciata frowned at her daughter. "That isn't kind," she reproved her.

Zenia stopped laughing abruptly. "Kind?" she snapped. "Was it kind for Franco to break Lucia's heart? I say, serves him right!"

"Who is Lucia?" asked Melanie.

"Lucia is my friend," Zenia told her. "She and Franco were going to be married as soon as they had saved some money. In those days he was just a mechanic. Every week he entered the state lottery, hoping to win enough to marry Lucia and have his own garage. And then he did win, a *huge* fortune. And suddenly there was Salvani, smarming around him and 'advising' him how to invest his money. And the next thing, Franco was engaged to Salvani's daughter."

"But surely, Salvani is rich enough not to have to do that?" said Melanie.

"A man with five daughters to provide for is never rich," Annunciata declared shrewdly.

"Lucia was so happy," Zenia said bitterly. "And now she weeps at night because she loved him and he betrayed her."

"I don't think it was his fault," Annunciata tried to soothe her daughter. "They were too strong for him."

Zenia shrugged. "Betrayal is betrayal. What difference does it make whose fault it is? But now I know he suffers I feel better. I'll tell Lucia, and perhaps she'll feel better, too."

"She won't," Melanie said. "Not if she loves him."

"Love," Zenia snorted. "It's better not to give a man too much love. He'll trample it underfoot because he can't think what else to do with it."

Melanie looked up, alerted by a note of despair in Zenia's manner that made her seem suddenly older than her years. Zenia caught her glance and assumed a cold, haughty air that warned her off.

"I think I'll go to bed," Melanie said. She was suddenly exhausted. She hurried upstairs and got into the shower, turning this way and that under the jet, feeling the refreshing water wash away the strains and tensions of the evening. But nothing could wash away the feeling of Vittorio's arm tight about her waist, or the imprint of his lips on hers, hot, fiercely passionate, angry and tender, both together. The magic had only lasted for a brief moment, but it had been long enough to hint at wonders to be discovered with this man—if only he hadn't forced himself to stop so soon.

When she'd finished showering, Melanie put the light out, threw open her windows and stood naked, facing the mountain. She raised her eyes to the summit, where the flames of Etna roared unceasingly, glowing red against the darkness. The cool night air caressed her flesh, but it didn't ease the fever that was raging through it. Only one man could do that.

Four

Next morning Melanie was on edge for Vittorio's appearance. As she ate her breakfast she was constantly alert for every sound outside, but when she'd finished the meal, there was still no sign of him.

She told herself that she wasn't really agitated, or at least, that her agitation had a rational basis. It was natural that she should want to know what had happened after they'd parted the night before, and it was inconsiderate of him not to hurry to tell her. But the burning memory on her lips made a mockery of this pretense. It had been such a fleeting kiss, awakening her senses but leaving them unsatisfied, and now she ached for him to come to her. She needed to look at him, to see how he looked at her. She wanted to know if his mouth, too, still felt the imprint of that stolen moment of passion. But the hours passed with dragging slowness, and Lady Melanie

Carlyle, who had always been able to whistle men to heel, found herself neglected.

She became angry. He had no right to absent himself without her permission. The estate could go to ruin while he neglected his duties.

But suddenly Vittorio was there inside her head, saying with quiet intensity that the land owned him and wouldn't let him go, and she was immediately ashamed of herself for the injustice she'd done him. She knew his deep love for Terrafiore. Whatever Salvani said, *that* was the true reason he was still here. Already she felt she understood him better than people he'd known all his life, because something in him had called to her the first moment they met and she had responded with fire.

She thought of his bleak life, living as a servant where he should have been the master, forced to stand by while an alien woman claimed the land he loved, and something stirred painfully in her heart. If only he would come soon, and they could talk about it. But he didn't come, and it was as though he had snubbed her. It would have been easy to ask Annunciata or Zenia where he might be, but the pride of generations of aristocracy held her back. She grew edgy, reading significance into trifles. When Zenia served her evening meal, Melanie could have sworn she saw a superior smile on her beautiful face, as though Zenia had the power to read her troubled heart. She decided it was time she pulled herself together, but when she went to bed, she was in a fever of discontent.

Next day there was still no sign of Vittorio. But then Leo went into town and returned saying that the whole of Fazzoli was buzzing with the news of Salvani's injuries. "They say he was set upon by a gang of ruffians who beat him up and left him to die," he declared, eyes wide.

Pride forgotten, Melanie went straight to the kitchen. "Where does Vittorio live?" she asked Annunciata tersely.

"He has a cottage higher up, *padrona*. Follow the road to the end of the olive groves, and take the track that you see there."

"Is there a village or just one cottage?"

"Just the one. You'll know it when you see it. It's called 'the island.'"

Leo saddled up for her and Melanie headed up the mountainside. She tried to reason away the dread in her heart, but instinct told her that Vittorio's disappearance was linked to Salvani's injuries, and as she climbed, she grew more fearful of what she would find.

Gradually, the lush fertility fell away, leaving rough countryside where little grew, until at last she reached a huge outcrop of rock that stood proudly alone. On the top, seeming to grow directly out of the rock, was a small cottage. Melanie tethered her horse and made her way up the narrow path that led to the front door, her heart beating with apprehension. The door was closed but not locked, and she hesitated for a moment before going inside.

She found herself in a large room with whitewashed walls, an open hearth surrounded by copper pots, and a wooden table on which stood a checkered cloth and a vase with cheerful yellow flowers. The floor was made of flagstones, covered with a rag rug. One wall was taken up by a crowded bookshelf, and when Melanie studied the books she found them to be works of poetry and philosophy. Here was another side to the man who was beginning to fascinate her.

She moved quickly to the door to the next room. It was forbiddingly closed, and she hesitated a long time before turning the handle and pushing it tentatively open. She discovered a bedroom that was sparsely furnished, with the large bed taking up most of the room. Melanie drew in her breath sharply at the sight of Vittorio on his back, his eyes closed, a sheet covering him up to his waist. When she crept a little closer she almost cried out at what she discovered.

His bare chest was covered in scratches and bruises. Bruises marked his face, and one corner of his mouth was swollen. He'd been in a fight and come out badly. Who knew what other injuries he had? She reached out a hand but drew back at the last minute, longing to touch him but somehow shy of doing so.

At that moment he opened his eyes and started violently at the sight of her. The abrupt movement made him wince and fall back on the bed. "What are you doing here?" he groaned.

"I had to find out what had happened to you. Vittorio, how badly are you hurt?"

"Not so badly," he said with a valiant effort at a shrug. "Only cuts and bruises."

"Just the same, I'm going to get a doctor for you."

"No," he said loudly. "Don't you dare do that. I forbid it, do you hear?"

"*Forbid?*" she echoed indignantly. It had been years since anyone had forbidden her to do anything.

"Yes, *your ladyship,*" he said in impeccable and ironic English. "Forbid. This doesn't concern you."

"Doesn't it? Are you saying it has nothing to do with Salvani?"

"To be sure, it's to do with Salvani, but it's nothing to do with *you*. After I left you the other night I went back and finished giving him the lesson in manners that I'd started."

"So you're the 'gang of ruffians' who set on him?"

Vittorio gave a crack of laughter and immediately winced. "Is that the story he's put out? Gang of ruffians! I like that. Yes, it was only me. I didn't do him any serious damage, but I spoiled his beauty a little. He won't show his face until the damage has faded. He set a couple of toughs on me in retaliation, but they were spineless. I saw them off." He flexed his hand where the knuckles were swollen, and grinned at her, actually cheerful. "Gang of ruffians," he repeated. "What a good joke!"

"I suppose it would be useless suggesting that you went to the police?" Melanie said crossly.

"Don't say things that will make me laugh, please," he begged. "It hurts too much. In this region a man settles his own disputes. It's simpler that way." He tried to raise himself, gasped and lay back.

"If you won't have a doctor, at least let me do something for you," she insisted.

He grinned. "Why must women insist on being ministering angels? You're as bad as Zenia."

"Has she been here?"

"Yes, she came up yesterday to find out what had become of me. Didn't she tell you?"

"No, she didn't mention it," Melanie said in a carefully colorless voice. Inwardly she was seething at Zenia for concealing what she knew. This was the reason for the superior smile last night.

"She should have done. I asked her to give you my apologies for not turning up for work." He sighed ruefully. "I had to be very firm to stop her taking over."

"Can't I do anything?" she asked, feeling rather foolish.

"Could you fetch me some wine?"

Following his directions, in the kitchen she found a trapdoor that led down into a cellar carved out of the rock. In contrast to the heat above, the air down there was chilly. With the aid of a torch, Melanie made out hams and cheeses hanging from the roof, and stone bottles containing oil and wine. A man could be self-sufficient here for some time, and that seemed all of a piece with what she already knew of Vittorio.

She took a bottle of wine and returned to him, collecting some glasses from the kitchen. He had managed to struggle up in bed, but from the defensive way he'd tucked the sheet in around him she guessed that he was naked. The thought brought back fiery memories of his kiss, his lips hard on hers for a brief, ecstatic moment, the casual power with which he'd held her off the ground, and heat surged up through her body with shocking suddenness.

She poured the wine, refusing to meet his eyes in case he read her weakness. She wanted to kiss him now, to lay her lips gently against his bruises and caress them softly. Her heart ached to see him hurt, and her flesh burned with the yearning to touch him. Instead, she had to sit there, pretending to be calm and composed, denying the fever that pervaded her at the thought of his nakedness, at the possibility of their nakedness together.

"Vittorio," she said abruptly, "why didn't you tell me you were Giorgio's son?"

She saw him stiffen and grow pale. "Who told you that?" he demanded in a bleak voice.

"Salvani, the other night. He said Giorgio and your mother were lovers, that it was common knowledge you're his son, and everyone had thought Terrafiore would be yours some day."

He looked at her cynically. "Are you sure that's quite what he said? Didn't he really tell you that *I* had expected Terrafiore to be mine, and not to trust me an inch because all I wanted was to steal it from you?"

"Well, he may have said something like that," she agreed awkwardly, "but I didn't believe him."

"Didn't you?" he asked bitterly. "I wonder."

"Do you think I'd trust anything that man said?"

"Not now perhaps, but then—"

"Well," she admitted, "it would have been easier if you'd told me yourself."

"Oh, yes," he said sarcastically. "I should have met you at the airport saying, *'Buon giorno, signorina.* I am Giorgio's bastard son and the man you have dispossessed.'"

She nodded. "Of course you couldn't."

A sudden darkness came into Vittorio's eyes. "Besides," he said heavily, "I'm not his son."

"But you look like him."

"I know. And his blood flows in my veins. He sent me abroad, and he favored me in many ways. And yet I am not his son." He met her eyes fiercely. "Do you know why? Because he never *called* me his son. Not once. Not a word. My mother told me it was true, but Giorgio never admitted it. All my life I waited to hear him say the words, and when he died without saying them—" Vittorio's mouth twisted "—I thought that he would give a sign in his will. Do you understand? It wasn't the property I cared about, but that my father should acknowledge me. But he never did."

He sighed. "So that's why you need not worry. I won't try to take Terrafiore from you, because in my heart I can't feel I have any right to it. All I ask of you is that you treat it well, and let me care for it."

She looked down at him in pity and horror at the suppressed pain in his voice. The bleak dignity with which he accepted his fate tore at her heart. "But must it matter so much whether he acknowledged you or not?" she said at last. "*I* think you're his son—"

"*You?*" he said angrily. "Who are you to think so? Do you think you have any standing in this matter?"

"I'm the legal owner of Terrafiore. I have that much standing. If I were to speak to the lawyer and—" She stopped with a gasp as Vittorio seized her wrist.

"Don't say it," he grated. "Do you imagine I could, *in honor,* take from you what *he* didn't chose to give me? If you think that, you insult me."

She looked at him in despair. The way he said "in honor" told her what she was up against. She would never break that stubborn Sicilian pride.

He released her wrist and lay back on the bed. His face was livid and perspiration stood out on his brow. "You'd better go now," he said.

"I can't leave you while you're ill," she said passionately. "Don't tell me you're all right. I don't believe it."

"All right, I'm not," he agreed wearily. "But you can't cure my sickness."

"I can try." She leaned over him, unable to resist touching his face. He looked up at her, and for an unguarded moment she saw in his eyes something that mirrored her own feelings. He was not as calm as he pretended. Their moment of passion still existed for him, too. He laid a hand over hers.

"Don't pity me," he whispered. "Don't ever dare to pity me. I'd hate you for it."

She tried to speak, but the burning look in his eyes silenced her. She felt as if she were choking. They came from different worlds. There could never be anything between them. She knew this, but the knowledge seemed to fade to nothing beside the electric current that flowed between them. Tremors ran through Melanie. Unable to stop herself, she took Vittorio's face between her hands and kissed him, gently at first, then passionately as she sensed his response. She felt his fingers running through her hair, his hand cupping her head, pulling her closer.

Then she was in his arms, lying beside him on the bed while his lips caressed hers purposefully and his tongue found its way into her mouth. She sighed with pleasure at the feeling, offering herself up to his sensual exploration, feeling darts of fire begin to go through her. She had a feeling of doing something utterly right and inevitable, something without which her life would be incomplete. He kissed her as though he already knew her, as though they'd been born part of each other and nothing was new, nothing unfamiliar. His tongue belonged in her mouth and his hands belonged on her body, just as hers belonged on him. Her fingers on his back were discovering the ripple of steely muscles beneath the smooth skin.

He began to kiss the line of her jaw. Despite his strength, there was incredible gentleness in his touch, his lips seeming to whisper against her skin as he sought the delicate place below her ear. She sighed with pleasure as his tongue made small flickers against her neck until he reached the hollow of her throat. She could feel the heat of his breath and just make out the murmuring sound he made against her skin.

"Fior di fuoco..."

"Vittorio..." she murmured in dazed delight, "Vittorio...yes...yes..."

He stiffened suddenly as if someone had struck him a blow. When he raised his head to look down at her, she saw that his eyes were as hazy with desire as her own must be, but somewhere far behind them a terrible struggle was taking place. He was fighting with himself not to let this happen, and he was a man who was strong enough to master his own will. Melanie put out pleading hands, imploring not to be denied the fulfilment to which this kiss must lead, but it was too late. She knew that when he raised his head defiantly, and she saw the grim set of his jaw. *"No,"* he said fiercely. "This will not happen. It *must* not."

"Vittorio," she whispered.

A shudder went through him. His eyes were full of shock, and he moved away as if trying to put a safe distance between them. "Sweet heaven, what am I doing?" he groaned. "I never meant—I have no right. You must go away—now."

"Why must I go?" she murmured dizzily.

"Why? Because you are so beautiful that I cannot look at you without wanting to touch you, and much more, because with you I have no control over myself. I forget that some things are impossible."

"Nothing is impossible," she said recklessly.

He gave a mirthless laugh. "It's only in fairy tales that the frog becomes a prince. Once I could have fought for you and made you mine. Now I haven't even the right to think of it."

"Then why did you kiss me that night you brought me home?" she flashed. "Did that *have* to be?"

"Yes," he growled. "Yes, it *had* to be. We couldn't know each other without that happening, even if only once. You know that's true...you felt it the first moment...as I did."

She nodded. "The first moment—but not only then. You shouldn't have kissed me that night if you didn't mean this to happen."

His mouth twisted. "You're right to reproach me. I couldn't stop myself then."

"And now you can?" she asked bitterly.

"Because I must. I called you *fior di fuoco*. It means fire flower. I've known you were the fire flower from the beginning."

"What does it mean?"

"It means danger," he said seriously.

Aching disappointment made her snap. "For heaven's sake, that sounds like a peasant superstition."

"But I am a peasant," he said simply. "Nor am I ashamed of it."

"Vittorio, I'm sorry, I didn't mean—"

"It's all right, I understand. But now you must understand that this thing between us must be killed while we still have time."

"Do we still have time? Do you really believe that?"

His face was haggard. "Yes."

"You're lying."

"Very well, I'm lying. Now *go*."

Always before, she'd been able to arrange things as she wanted them. Now she understood that she was dealing with a man as uncompromising as the land that lay between them. "All right, I'll go—for now," she said in a trembling voice. "But I don't believe that anything is impossible."

"You must. We must both accept it if we're to stay sane. For the sake of the land. For the sake of Terrafiore, that will be here when you and I are long forgotten, *padrona*."

It hurt that he should call her that now, but it would be useless to say more. She rose from the bed where only a few minutes ago she'd been close to ecstasy and forced herself to go to the door. Once she looked back at Vittorio and discovered his face bleak but set.

Reluctantly she left him, but as she rode away, she swore that this wouldn't be the finish. Every part of her throbbing body told her that it couldn't end this way. Vittorio had awakened a desire in her that was unlike anything she'd ever felt before in her life, a desire that would torment her until it was satisfied. She wanted him, and Lady Melanie Carlyle was used to getting what she wanted.

Zenia was waiting in the doorway for her when she got home. Her eyes were brilliant with suspicion, as though she guessed where Melanie had been. "Signor Doletti came to see you," she said.

Melanie jumped down from the mare and tossed the reins to Leo. "Who is Signor Doletti?"

"He's an important man in Fazzoli. He runs the bank and has control of several businesses. He's one of the organizers of the festival of Santa Marina. It's a big holiday, with a funfair and puppet shows, and a procession through the town. People come from miles around to see it."

"It sounds delightful, but why did Signor Doletti come to see me?"

"Because the festival is next week and the owner of Terrafiore always leads the procession on horseback. Last year your aunt asked Vittorio to do it for her." She added casually, "I said he'd do it this year, too."

Melanie stared at her. "You said *what?*"

"Leading the procession is a man's job," Zenia asserted calmly. "It's always been that way. It would be unthinkable for a woman."

"Not this woman. And whatever I decide, *you* do not speak for me."

"I was only trying to help you," Zenia said. "You don't know our ways. You'd cause a scandal."

"Is this the twentieth century, or isn't it?" Melanie demanded crossly.

Zenia looked at her strangely. "You don't actually mean to do it?"

Melanie ground her teeth. "If I wish to, I will."

Zenia shrugged. "Vittorio won't like it."

Melanie drew in her breath and strove to speak without losing her temper. "Vittorio doesn't make my decisions any more than you do," she said firmly. "This discussion is closed."

She strode into the house, thoroughly angry. Zenia's insolence was beyond bearing and her confident assertion of Vittorio's wishes raised up a picture in Melanie's mind: the two of them in his cottage yesterday, discussing her, agreeing that she didn't belong. Halfway up the stairs she stopped, then impulsively she ran back down and out into the yard. "Saddle me a fresh horse," she ordered Leo.

"But *padrona,*" he protested, "the only other horse is Zeus, and he's not a lady's horse."

"And just what does that mean?"

"He belonged to the late master. Only Vittorio ever dares to exercise him."

"Well, Vittorio will be away for a few days, so saddle him up for me," she commanded.

She was beginning to be more amused then annoyed. She'd ridden fiery animals all her life and the concept of a 'lady's horse' struck her as being straight out of the nineteenth century. She understood Leo's apprehension when Zeus was brought out to her, saddled. He was an ugly-looking, raw-boned piebald whose big, glowing eyes contained a challenge. The minute she mounted him he kicked, but Melanie was ready and brought him firmly under control at once. A murmur of admiration went around the workmen who had gathered curiously. He tried to unseat her a couple of times but failed, and she could sense him relaxing, as though accepting her authority. She permitted herself a little smile of satisfaction, which widened when she glimpsed Zenia watching her from the shadows of the cloister, a scowl on her face. "Now I'm going into town," she said, and turned Zeus out of the courtyard into the countryside.

Almost at once he took off at a gallop and it took all her strength to hold him, but she managed it and reached Fazzoli in triumph. An astonished woman indicated the way to the bank, and when she'd found someone to take care of Zeus, she strode in and asked to see Signor Doletti. As soon as she gave her name, doors were opened for her, and in a few moments she was in a cool marble-floored office, surveying a dapper little man over his huge desk.

When he learned her errand, he exclaimed with delight. "This makes everything perfect. The procession is not the same without the owner of Terrafiore."

"You don't think people will mind about my being a woman?"

He shrugged. "It's an innovation, but we must move with the times, must we not? I think it's a wonderful idea. Besides, it's your right."

"I'm glad you think so. That's not the reaction I've had so far."

Doletti laughed. "You mean Zenia? Yes, she was in a great hurry to tell me that you wouldn't even consider it."

"Was she indeed?" Melanie echoed grimly.

"I must say, I'd have been surprised if you'd let her get away with that. I've always heard that English women are very independent. You haven't disappointed me. I suggest you come to lunch with my family on the day, and I can explain everything to you then.''

"Thank you. I think that sounds delightful." She rose and shook his hand firmly. "I'm really looking forward to this festival."

Five

****

Vittorio returned to work next day. Melanie was out riding and came back to find him standing outside the boundary wall, watching her approach, with an expression that spelled trouble. "We must talk," he said grimly as he took her bridle.

"Very well, let's talk," Melanie said. "But I won't change my mind."

He tossed the reins to Leo and indicated the house with his head, in a gesture that was as unconsciously imperious as any of Melanie's. She followed him into the large living room that was in near darkness because the shutters were drawn. He turned to face her in the gloom. "Will you at least listen to me? What you're proposing to do is unsuitable."

"Because I'm a woman?"

"Partly, yes."

"How old-fashioned!"

"Very well. Call me old-fashioned, but try to understand one thing. This is not a society in which women take the lead."

"And this," she said, pointing to herself, "is not a woman who meekly sits back and lets a man do what she is capable of doing for herself."

"The procession has never before been led by a woman. Dulcie understood."

She gave a grim laugh. "So it was you who talked Dulcie into backing out. I might have guessed. Well, the difference between her and me is that she came from an earlier generation of women, one that still believed in being deferential to men."

"The difference between her and you," he responded bitingly, "is that she'd lived in Sicily long enough to learn its ways, and respect them. She wasn't arrogant."

"Arrogant?" she echoed, stung.

"What else do you call someone who storms into an unfamiliar society like a bull in a china shop, and assumes she knows it all?"

"Bull in a—? Knows it—when I've meekly accepted everything you've said about Terrafiore—?"

"Am I supposed to thank you for recognizing your own ignorance?" he demanded furiously. "You have no choice but to let me run the estate. But in everything else you act first and think afterward. Look at the way you rushed off to Doletti without talking to me. I could have warned you he's hand in glove with Salvani. He's a banker, and Salvani can't buy this place without his help."

She shrugged, refusing to let him see that this disturbed her. "So Doletti regards it as a good investment for the bank. Very sensible of him."

"Salvani is also one of the organizers of this festival. Did you know that?"

"No—but it doesn't mean they're hand in glove. What do I have to fear from Salvani? He can't attack me in full view of everyone."

He ran a hand worriedly through his hair. "It's because I don't know what he's going to do that I'm worried. For pity's sake, be sensible about this."

"And give Salvani the satisfaction of seeing me back out? No way. Would you do that?"

"That's different," he said firmly.

"The hell it is!"

In the poor light, she could just make out Vittorio's eyes kindling. "Why can't you listen to good advice?" he raged.

"Because I don't like being told what to do," she said firmly. "Just who do you think you are to give me orders?"

"I'm someone who's trying to stop you taking stupid risks in a situation you don't understand—someone who— *oh, amor di Dio.*" The last exclamation was uttered almost under his breath, and before she knew what he meant to do, he'd pulled her hard against him and crushed her lips with his own.

The sudden action, coming with no warning, stunned her. As her reactions returned to life she realized that Vittorio was still furiously angry and this was simply a different way of showing it. He was kissing her fiercely, silencing argument with the erotic power of his lips, and that power was overwhelming. It made her feel as if she were melting inside.

When she could speak, she whispered mockingly, "And you were so determined to be strong!"

"I meant it, but you would try the patience of a saint," he growled just before his mouth covered hers again.

Joy flooded her at the thought that Vittorio couldn't resist her, for she knew she could never resist him. She let her fingers trace patterns on the back of his neck and find their way into his hair, all the time molding her body against his, aching for him. It was shameless, but that was how he made her feel. "Vittorio..." she whispered, "why do we fight?"

"We fight about nothing—nothing that matters." Then, with sudden, hoarse urgency, he murmured, "I don't want to fight you." He slid his tongue into her mouth and began to explore her with delicate skill, flickering against the silky inside skin and triggering flames of delight that roared along her nerves. She made a soft sound of pleasure and felt his hand cup her head, the fingers weaving into her hair, which had been pinned up for riding, pulling it down until it streamed over her shoulders.

Melanie let her head fall back, looking up into his face with hazy, desire-filled eyes. She was on the verge of yielding to him utterly. At that moment he could have had her body, her heart and soul—or her agreement to do whatever he wanted. Then suddenly, her dizzied senses became aware of a presence in the shadows near the door. She tensed, saying, "Who's there?"

Vittorio turned swiftly, yet not swiftly enough to see anyone. He strode to the door but returned a moment later. "There was no one there. You imagined it." He ran a hand through his hair. His face was haggard with strain. "Still, I shouldn't have kissed you here. It was indiscreet. Are you angry with me?"

She shook her head. The blood was still pounding deliciously through her veins and she was almost beyond words. No other man's kiss had ever affected her as Vittorio's did, and she hadn't wanted to stop, but there was danger in the way he could make her want to abandon all caution. She drew a ragged breath, trying to force her heart to calm its beating. A sudden impulse made her throw open the shutters, letting brilliant light stream into the room and revealing her to herself in a small mirror that hung on the wall. Her hair was tousled and her eyes had a dazed look that showed only too clearly how she'd been slipping out of her own control and into Vittorio's.

He spoke tenderly. "Will you tell Doletti yourself, or would you prefer me to do it for you?"

"Doletti?" For a moment she could barely recall the name. "Tell him what?"

"That you won't be in the procession."

Her head snapped up as cold disillusion washed over her. "So that was why—?" She drew in her breath. "That was just your method of getting your own way, wasn't it?"

He smiled. "I prefer it to arguing. Or rather, it's the best way of settling an argument. Why should we fight about something that doesn't really matter to you?"

"What matters to me," she said, speaking with difficulty, "is that you should have the infernal gall to imagine you can sweep me off my feet with a kiss, and then walk all over me."

He groaned in exasperation. "I'm trying to protect you. If that's your idea of walking all over you—"

"Vittorio, listen. Don't protect me. Don't make my decisions for me. And above all, don't patronize me. My mind is made up. Is that clear?"

"Perfectly clear," he said, tight-lipped. "And I hope you don't regret it."

"You mean you hope that I *do* regret it, so that you can be proved right."

He glared at her before slamming one fist into the other hand and stalking out.

In the week that was left before the festival, they maintained a cool and utterly correct relationship. Vittorio presented himself every morning to explain his plans for the day and ask if they met with the *padrona's* approval. Melanie assured him that they did, and usually that was the last she saw of him until the next day.

The more she thought of it, the more convinced she became that it had been Zenia who'd stood in the shadows, watching them kiss. She went about with a drawn face and her eyes were wretched. Yet occasionally Melanie caught a malicious smile on her face, a smile that was wiped off when she realized she was being watched.

On the day of the festival, Leo brought Rosa to her, saddled up. She'd given everyone the day off to go to Fazzoli, and she could tell they were all eager to see her off and begin enjoying themselves. But one face was missing.

She finally ran Vittorio to earth in the room that housed the olive press, where he was dealing with a repair. "Aren't you at least going to wish me luck?" she asked, holding out her hand.

He didn't seem to see it. "If you choose to behave foolishly, is there any point in wishing you good luck?" he asked, looking at her with chilly eyes.

"I'd hoped we might bury the hatchet today. Aren't you coming to the festival?" For he alone wasn't in traditional costume.

"I have work to attend to," he said briefly.

She concealed her disappointment to say wryly, "I'd have sworn you'd have come along to keep a watchful eye over me and pick up the pieces."

"But that would be to patronize you," he pointed out.

Her hand fell to her side. "You're quite right. In that case, I'll be off. Don't stay here working. Take the day off, like the others."

He didn't reply and she walked out, feeling his cold eyes on her until the last moment. A few minutes later she was on her way to Fazzoli on Rosa's back.

Doletti's house was a few hundred yards out of town. To get to it, Melanie had to pass a small funfair that had been set up on a stretch of open land next to Fazzoli. There were a few carousels, but she noticed that what drew most attention were the booths with puppet shows depicting heavily armed knights engaged in noisy battle. She stopped to look and bought a sticky sweet from a nearby stall, but the first piece she broke off was too rich for her palate, and she distributed the rest to a little crowd of eager children.

Doletti's house was fronted by a large courtyard that was already crowded with gaily painted carts. Melanie could see Doletti, dressed in a colorful, elaborate version of the black, decorated peasant costume, which overwhelmed his slight frame. He waved when he saw her and held the horse's head while she dismounted.

"This is Benedetta, my wife," he said, introducing a large woman, also dressed in traditional peasant garb. Melanie shook hands and looked about her, realizing suddenly that all the women were attired in this way, although some of them had added expensive jewellery, as if reminding the world that they weren't really peasants.

"I'm going to look rather odd," she said, glancing down at her severe riding attire.

"But I have a costume for you," Benedetta said. "You will look magnificent."

She began to show Melanie around the *carretti,* the little carts, all hand painted with detailed scenes showing Sicily's eventful history. "The past is never dead for us," she explained. "On this cart, you see our knights battling against the Saracen invaders, and here is Garibaldi and his thousand men, landing at Marsala."

Melanie studied the *carretti* in genuine fascination. They were real works of art, decorated with enormous skill and delicacy, not just at the sides, but all over the wheels and along the shafts. Although old, they were in perfect condition, cleaned and restored with love.

"Buon giorno, signorina."

Melanie stiffened at the sound of a remembered voice and looked up to find Salvani standing there, gigantic and absurd in his elaborate peasant garb.

"Buon giorno," she said stiffly, but added no further comment, hoping he would take the hint.

Instead he seized her hand and declared, "It's a real pleasure to see you here today."

She studied his face, which still bore a few yellow marks. "I see you're up and about again after being waylaid by a 'gang of ruffians,' " she said ironically. She turned her wrist swiftly so that she could view the back of his hand. The two little wounds she'd made with her scissors had healed but were still visible.

Salvani's smile wavered for just a second, but he held it in place by force of will. "It takes more than that to defeat me, *signorina,*" he said softly.

"We'll see, won't we?" she murmured back.

Irena appeared and greeted Melanie like a long-lost friend. "How happy I am that we can now put right the tragic misunderstanding that has marred our friendship," she said earnestly.

"Was there a misunderstanding?" Melanie asked coolly.

"My husband has told me how stupidly he behaved when he drove you home, how he stopped the car to talk, and you took fright and thought he meant—well, never mind. He meant well but he's a foolish man. But you were foolish, too, to rush out of the car in the darkness. Of course he had to run after you, to stop you getting lost."

So that was the gloss they were going to put on it. Melanie regarded them both cynically. *"Signora,"* she said at last, "I came here today to enjoy myself, as I'm sure you did. Shall we leave it at that?"

"Of course! It's so lovely to know we're all friends again," Irena said determinedly.

Melanie gave her a brief, artificial smile and turned away.

Benedetta took her upstairs to dress. Her costume consisted of a wide green embroidered skirt, topped off by a white blouse with plenty of frills over the bosom and on the sleeves. Over this was worn a black velvet waistcoat, cut away at the top so that the front met only under the breasts. There was a white apron, also heavily frilled and embroidered, and a green cloak that clasped around her neck. The whole appearance was traditional and romantic, and Melanie loved it on sight.

When it was on, the black waistcoat emphasized her tiny waist and high breasts, and she knew she looked good. She couldn't help thinking of Vittorio, wondering what he was doing now and whether he would think she looked beautiful.

Lunch was laid out in the open, on tables covered with snowy cloths and festooned with garlands of leaves. All Fazzoli's prominent citizens were there. Salvani and his wife were at the top table, with Melanie, but far enough away for her to pretend they weren't there. Benedetta, seated beside her, gave her a rundown on her neighbors and insisted that soon she would give a little party in her honor, "so that you may meet the proper people."

For some reason the words brought Vittorio into Melanie's thoughts again. It was strange, she thought, how every tiny thing could remind her of him. Nobody in this wealthy, overdressed crowd would think him a "proper person," and yet, stubborn, difficult and prickly though he was, he'd captured her imagination and wouldn't release her.

"Lucia," Benedetta called, "some more wine over here."

A young woman appeared quietly at the table and began to refill glasses. As she finished and moved away, Melanie saw her look quickly at the next table, where Franco sat meekly beside his overdressed wife, who was hectoring him in loud tones. An expression of anguish flitted across the servant's face and was gone. The next moment she was going about her duties again, her face impassive.

So this was the Lucia that Zenia had spoken of, Melanie realized, the one who'd been betrothed to Franco and had seen him swallowed alive by the predatory Salvanis. Glancing at the young man, she saw that, despite his subdued demeanor, his eyes kept following Lucia. She felt sad for them both.

At last lunch was over and it was time for the procession to begin. A crowd was beginning to congregate. Horses and donkeys were put between the shafts of the *carretti,* and the town band made tuneless but enthusiastic noises. A huge plaster statue of Saint Marina was waiting to be hoisted onto the shoulders of six carriers, and immediately behind her, a gathering of excited children were fitting themselves into the green skin that represented the dragon the saint had overcome before being martyred. "Where will I find Rosa?" Melanie asked.

"You won't need her," Benedetta said. "We have a special horse for you, one who's used to a sidesaddle. You can ride sidesaddle, of course?"

Melanie nodded. She had sometimes ridden sidesaddle in county horse shows in England and felt she could acquit herself reasonably well. Her mount turned out to be a gray stallion, extravagantly decked out with flowers, bells and ribbons. He looked enormously strong and was much larger than she would normally have chosen to ride, but he paid no attention to the gathering din in the yard, not even when the band's drummer began to thump loudly a few feet away.

"His name is Rocco, and he's been specially trained to cope with noisy crowds," Benedetta explained, "so all this doesn't bother him."

"But where do I go?" Melanie asked. "I'm leading the procession, but I don't know the way."

"Ride straight along the high street as far as it goes, until you reach the little patch of wasteland at the other side of Fazzoli," Benedetta explained. "Someone there will take the horse."

Melanie bowed her head to receive the chaplet of flowers that Benedetta set on it, then mounted to the accompaniment of a cheer. Salvani, who was talking to the band leader, raised his head and smiled at her in a way she found unnerving. There was something pleased and malicious in his look, and for a moment, she nearly expected to discover that he'd substituted a half-wild animal, but Rocco stood in docile silence as she settled herself in the saddle and the rest of the procession fell in behind. Doletti raised his arm to give the signal, and they were off.

Crowds had already streamed out to line the route for the few hundred yards into town. They waved and clapped at the sight of Melanie mounted on the gaily caparisoned stallion, and she grew sufficiently confident to wave back, while the band oompahed resolutely, if inaccurately, behind her. She relaxed. It was clear she'd been worrying about nothing.

She reached the edge of town. The crowds were heavier now, full of people who'd come from Catania and all the surrounding countryside, so that little Fazzoli seemed ready to burst at the seams. People packed the pavements, spilling over into the main street that wound through the town. Bunting hung overhead. Windows were open, with more people crowding them to get a look at the procession below, laughing, cheering and tossing down flowers that landed in Melanie's path, making her realize the value of having a trained horse, for Rocco never flinched.

The band had come to the end of its first piece. There was a brief pause, then the notes of the next tune floated into the air. At once Melanie felt the stallion shift beneath her, and the next second Rocco had reared up on his hind legs. Taken by surprise, she was almost thrown, but instinctively she tightened her legs on the sidesaddle and fought grimly to stay on. It was touch and go, with the unfamiliar saddle making it more difficult, but she managed to keep her seat, praying that Rocco would drop his front hooves soon. After what seemed an eternity, he did so, and Melanie breathed again, wondering what could have made the animal behave so oddly.

But almost immediately Rocco reared up again. This time Melanie clung on more firmly, but the swaying dislodged her chaplet of flowers, so that it slid sideways and hung down drunkenly over one eye, prompting a burst of laughter from the crowd. She ground her teeth until Rocco dropped his hooves again, and reached up to adjust the chaplet. But no sooner had she done so than Rocco reared up a third time. This time the laughter was a roar.

Melanie counted eight beats of the music until the horse's hooves touched the ground again, realizing suddenly that it had always been exactly eight beats. Of course, she thought, Rocco was responding to the music. If she could just cling on until the end of this tune, she'd be safe.

Mercifully the band reached the end at that moment. Then, after another brief pause, they swung into a cheery march. Rocco pricked up his ears and promptly began to turn in a rightward circle. Nothing Melanie could do would stop him. The crowd rocked, both at the horse's antics and at the rider's discomfiture. She set her jaw, refusing to let them see her anger and embarrassment. The truth was becoming clear. Rocco's training must have been in a circus, and now she knew why Salvani had been talking to the band leader. He'd set her up for this, to punish her for humiliating him. He knew the tunes that would make Rocco respond, and he'd arranged to have them played. As Rocco swung around to face the procession, Melanie got a brief glimpse of Salvani on a wagon just behind the band, his cruel face lit up with glee. And there in the crowd was Zenia, beside herself with laughter. Melanie's cheeks burned, and she was glad that Vittorio couldn't see her looking such a fool.

The march finished and Rocco settled down again, but Melanie's relief was short-lived, for the band immediately began to reprise the first tune, causing the stallion to rear up again. Melanie hung on grimly, wondering how much longer there was to go, but as she felt herself descending again there was a splat from just behind her, loud enough to make itself heard over the din. Rocco gave a shrill whinny at the feel of a sharp stone hitting his rump, and the next moment he'd broken into a gallop and was tearing out of town at top speed.

It took all Melanie's concentration to keep her seat. She hauled on the bit, but Rocco had a mouth of leather and she could make no impression on him whatever. She was aware of the countryside streaming past her in a blur, of the town falling away and the land becoming rough. They were climbing, but Rocco's speed didn't diminish. In the whistling of the wind, Melanie wasn't sure if she heard or only imagined the sound of someone calling her name, and she didn't dare look back.

But gradually she became aware of other hoofbeats close by. She risked a brief glance over her shoulder and saw Vittorio, mounted on Zeus, slowly gaining on her. His jaw was set grimly as he urged his mount faster in a desperate attempt to catch up. Then his eyes widened in horror and he signaled frantically for Melanie to look ahead. She did so, just in time to see the boulders piled up ahead, before Rocco took off and soared over them. With no idea what lay on the other side, Melanie prayed as she'd never prayed before, and somehow they landed safely. Then Vittorio was there beside her again, reaching for her bridle, but Rocco eluded him, thundering on with untiring energy.

By now they were higher up the slope of Etna than Melanie had ever been before. Here the land was stony, threatening her with serious injury if she should lose her seat. She was exhausted and aching all over, wondering how much longer she could last, and still there was no sign of the end.

But then it happened. Rocco stumbled and lurched sideways. He managed to regain his balance, but for Melanie it was the last straw. She was almost numb with strain and weariness, and after having clung on through every danger, now she simply slid off. For a moment the earth spun and the stones whirled up to meet her. Then there was a bump, she gasped for breath, closed her eyes and opened them almost at once, to find herself sprawled on a patch of rough grass baked brown by the heat.

The next moment Vittorio had flung himself down beside her. *"Melanie..."* he cried with a jagged edge on his voice. *"Oh, mio Dio!"*

"I'm all right," she said shakily. "I don't think anything's broken."

For answer he took her into his arms and pulled her against him. Melanie held on to him, eager to feel the welcome solidity of his body after the battering she'd taken. "I'm all right," she said again.

But he seemed not to hear her. He was rocking her gently back and forth, murmuring, "You might have been killed, and it would have been my fault. I should have stopped you, but I was mad with pride and jealousy...forgive me!"

She looked up into his face, struck with wonder at a note in his voice she'd never heard before. "Vittorio..." she whispered.

"Tell me that you are not hurt," he begged. Before she could answer, he seized her hand and swore violently at the sight of the grazes. "I will kill that man," he vowed.

He rose, lifting her in his arms, and began to walk. She caught a glimpse of Rocco galloping into the distance, but when she turned her head to follow him, her muscles protested and she gave up. She was all aches and pains, but that was nothing compared to the heady excitement of being in Vittorio's arms, where every instinct was telling her she belonged.

Six

After a while "the island" came into view. Vittorio climbed the steep path to the summit of the rock, kicked open the front door and carried her into the bedroom, where he set her down on the bed and sat beside her, holding her tightly in his arms and rocking to and fro. At last he laid her down on the pillows and seemed to become self-conscious. "I'll get some water," he said. "Stay there."

But when she was alone, Melanie got stiffly to her feet and studied her disheveled appearance in the mirror on the pine dressing table. The lovely costume was badly torn in several places, and the flesh beneath was already showing signs of bruises. She removed the black velvet waistcoat and raised the white blouse, twisting so that she could see her back. The movement made her wince, and she gasped aloud, clutching the edge of the dressing table.

Vittorio returned at that moment and scowled when he saw her. "I told you to rest," he said.

"I want to see my back," she insisted.

"Here..." He came behind her and raised the blouse gently lifting it right over her head and surveying the expanse of silky, bare skin, for she wasn't wearing a bra. For a tense moment there was silence, then he said in a strained voice, "There are no marks on your back."

He didn't move, didn't touch her, but Melanie could feel his hot breath against her bare shoulders and knew that he was fighting a colossal inner battle. His self-control was slipping away fast, and every harsh, ragged breath brought him closer to the moment of abandon. The knowledge of just how badly he wanted her was an unbearable erotic tease, starting fires raging through her flesh, making her yearn for the touch he was struggling not to give.

Slowly she turned to face him, letting her arms fall to her sides. He seemed stunned as he looked at her, and her aches faded beside the tremors of excitement that were coursing through her body. They had their beginnings in his expression, whose hungry urgency excited her. His burning eyes were caressing her breasts, and the consciousness made her nipples stand up proud and hard.

"Melanie..." His whisper was almost inaudible, but she heard it, "Melanie..."

Suddenly he lost the battle and seized her in his arms, pulling her against him and dropping his head until his lips touched hers. The hunger she'd seen in his eyes was multiplied a thousandfold in his kiss. All restraint was gone now as he kissed her with driving purpose, moving his firm lips over her willing mouth. She clasped him to her eagerly, feeling the thunder of his heart against her own through the thin cotton of his shirt. Beneath her hands, the muscles of his back were hard. The legs pressed against hers were steely with taut muscles, and she could feel a trembling in his whole body that matched her own.

Her head was on his shoulder in an attitude of abandon. She was freely offering herself up to him, driven by the desire that had tortured her since he'd kissed her on horseback. How long ago that seemed, and how much more thrilling was the slow, deliberate intent with which his lips caressed her at this moment. He kissed her like a man possessed, and everything in her responded wholeheartedly. When his tongue sought a way between her lips, she let them fall apart for him, wanting to feel him inside her, a promise and an echo of the deeper union that must come soon.

He lifted her and laid her on the bed, running his hands feverishly over her. She responded by working on his shirt, until it came off and she too could enjoy the feel of bare skin, smooth beneath her hands. His shoulders and chest were heavy with muscles that tapered down to a taut waist and flat stomach, and Melanie explored his shape with sensuous pleasure, rejoicing in the freedom to touch him as she wanted. She'd had to deny herself the pleasure for so long.

Vittorio dropped his head and laid his lips reverently against one breast, cupping its fullness in one hand. Slowly he began to caress it with his tongue, sending forks of fire through her. She let out a sigh of pure delight, willing this to go on forever—then changing her mind at once, for she wanted far more. This was just a beginning, a slow erotic introduction that must lead to the total intimacy her flesh craved. To have his head against her breast, his lips inflicting sweet torture on the proud, upstanding nipple, that was pleasure. But there would be more than mere pleasure in their mating. She understood that by instinct, although what more there would be was still a mystery. She knew only that the exploration of that mystery was the most vital thing in life, and nothing could stop her.

She reached for the fastening of her skirt, but Vittorio was already there, releasing it and slipping the material down over her hips. Her slip followed it, then her panties, and then she was naked. Vittorio moved quickly to throw off his trousers, revealing that he had nothing underneath. Melanie regarded him in wonder, awed by the sight of so much male beauty. His compact, muscular body had not an ounce of unnecessary flesh, but was firm and lean from the vigorous outdoor life he led. His flat stomach, narrow hips and powerful thighs filled her with delighted anticipation, as did the uncompromising urgency of his proud manhood.

But great as his need was, he had the control to delay, discovering the secrets of her slim body slowly, as if savoring a treasure that had become his by an unexpected miracle. His hands worked directly with the earth, and the hours of labor were reflected in their hardness. Yet his touch was incredibly gentle as he caressed and teased her, making her gasp with the games he knew how to play.

"You are the fire flower," he murmured against her silky skin, "so white and delicate, but with fire at your heart. I want your fire ... say it is mine...."

"All yours," she whispered in a daze of passion. "Yours to take..."

Her loins were throbbing with the powerful urge to feel him there. Nothing in her whole life had ever been like the craving for this man, the wanting, needing, yearning ache of deprivation and blazing desire that was concentrated between her legs in a delicious torture of longing that only he could satisfy.

"Yes...mine," he growled, "you are mine because you had to be...."

He moved over her and she opened her thighs to receive him, meeting him halfway as he entered her. She smiled with fulfillment as she felt him claim her deeply, then again, thrusting into her with a sweet piercing movement that vibrated through her flesh and made her cry aloud with ecstasy. He was looking down intently at her face, smiling deep into her eyes, communicating with her silently, turning the act into more than a physical mating, making it a true union.

The pleasure mounted. She was losing control. But his eyes were still there, smiling gently, giving her a safety to cling to as she felt herself go spinning away into darkness. But even in the darkness he was there, holding her, possessing her, whispering, "*La mia fior di fuoco,* my fire flower." The whisper was still in her ears as she returned to the light of common day to find that they had become their single selves again and that to be apart from him made her ache with desolation.

But the way he gathered her into his arms told her that he too suffered from their separation, and the knowledge eased her heart. She lay contentedly on his chest for a long while, happy simply to be close to him.

"Say you forgive me," he said huskily at last.

"For what?" she asked, trying to focus her mind.

"For what happened to you today, for letting you get hurt."

"There's nothing for me to forgive, Vittorio. I should have listened to you."

He turned, making her lie back against the pillows, and looked down at her before saying, "I should have stopped you from going, by force if necessary."

She raised her eyebrows quizzically. "Don't be so sure. I'm not easy to force."

He smiled and her heart lurched. "So I'm beginning to learn. But to protect you, there is nothing I wouldn't resort to." He looked at her grazed hand again and dropped his head to caress the sore place with his lips. "I should have locked you up before letting this happen," he said with perfect seriousness.

"Indeed?"

He smiled again. "We could have argued about it afterward." He rose and pulled an old cotton robe about him.

"Where are you going?" she asked.

"I brought you here to take care of you, not take advantage of you."

"'Take advantage of me.' What a delightful, old-fashioned expression."

"Sicily is an old-fashioned place, and perhaps it's none the worse for that," he said seriously. "Now I'm really going to take care of you."

He went into the kitchen and returned after a few minutes with a bowl of hot water. While she was sponging her grazes, he disappeared again, and when he came back he brought coffee, bread and oil.

"Well, I guess you were right," she sighed as they picnicked together on the bed. "Salvani had it in for me, and he managed to destroy my dignity very effectively in front of all Fazzoli."

"There's more to it than that," Vittorio said, frowning. "That horse is dangerous. He belongs to a circus that comes around these parts every year. His owners ought to retire him, but they can't afford to. He was well trained, but he's become very unpredictable. That's why, although he stood up well to the crowds, he lost control when he felt the stone on his rump."

"So that's what it was. I only heard it."

"Yes, I saw it delivered by a little boy with a catapult." Vittorio sighed unhappily. "I'm afraid he's a cousin of Zenia's."

"You think she put him up to it?" Melanie demanded. And then a memory came back to her, of how Zenia had told Doletti that she wouldn't ride, without consulting her, of her own anger, and her insistence on riding. "Yes," she said slowly. "Zenia made sure I didn't refuse. She knew about that horse, too."

Vittorio sighed. "She's taken an unreasoning dislike to you and it's made her act stupidly. I'm sure she didn't mean to endanger you. She just didn't think. Don't worry. I'll talk to her like a big brother and make her see sense."

Melanie was sure Zenia regarded him as anything but a brother, but she let it go at that. For now she just wanted to enjoy being here with Vittorio, free of the usual constraints of their respective positions. She got up and began to look around the room. Like the main room, it was sparsely furnished, except for a bookshelf whose contents were unexpectedly sophisticated. Vittorio watched her, smiling.

"The complete works of Shakespeare," she said, running her fingers down the spine, "and Milton, and Winston Churchill's speeches."

"I love your language at its best," he admitted. "When I was traveling I spent more time in England than any other country."

"That's why you speak such good English?"

He grinned with a gleam of mischief she'd never seen in him before. "That's always surprised you, hasn't it? You expected a Sicilian to 'spikka da English.' When I was in England I worked in a restaurant, and one day the boss called me over and said, 'Vittorio, the customers don't like the way you speak English.' I said, 'But my English is very good.' And he said 'That's what's wrong. You don't speak English like an Italian.' He wanted me to give a performance—'Pliss *signore,* you wanta I show-a you-a de table? My English, she is good, *sì?*'" Vittorio's imitation of bad stage Italian was so wickedly accurate that Melanie burst out laughing, and he laughed with her.

"I refused," he added, "so the boss threw me out. I had to sleep in the open for a few nights, but it didn't matter."

"No, I don't suppose much matters to you beside your stubborn pride," Melanie said mischievously.

He shrugged. "I'm not an organ grinder's monkey."

She nodded. It was impossible to imagine Vittorio yielding in inch where his self-respect was concerned. "Where was this?" she asked. "In London?"

"No, in Stratford-upon-Avon. I was there for the Shakespeare. I saw *Romeo and Juliet* three times, and marveled that an Englishman could understand Italians so well."

"I've never got on with that play," Melanie admitted. "I always feel that they could have managed to be together if they'd shown a bit more common sense."

"There speaks an Englishwoman," he mocked. "Common sense! What does that have to do with it? If you came from these parts you'd know how love and death and fate can be entangled. Some loves are not meant to be."

At another time she might have argued, but just now she was entranced by the sight of him leaning back on the bed, naked except for the robe that barely covered him. The shape of his strong, sturdy body had teased and fascinated her from the start, and the need to explore it had been growing in her by degrees until today, when it had exploded into uncontrollable passion. The feel of him was still there on her palms, in the soft flesh of her breasts, between her legs and deep in her loins. The memory of that thrusting power made a new surge of warmth go through her, bringing a soft pink flush to her cheeks. She looked away, embarrassed by her own pagan wantonness, but almost at once she looked back, met his eyes and knew it was the same with him. He knew what was happening inside her, because it was happening to him, too. The desire that had brought them together had been slaked only briefly, and now it was throbbing with fresh force through their bodies, urging them toward union, making it impossible for them to refuse.

He was smiling at her, refusing to make the first move, challenging her to make it. At last she did, leaning forward and pulling the string on his robe, so that the front fell apart and she saw what she needed to know. He wanted her as badly as she wanted him. She reached out and touched him softly and felt the uncontrollable response in his flesh.

He threw off the robe and pushed her back onto the bed. His eyes were ardent as he lightly stroked her face with the tips of his fingers, letting one finger drift slowly over her mouth and tracing the outline of her lips. At once it started again, the irresistible delight that spread out to every part of her, flooding her with warmth and anticipation. The sensation of that feather-light touch on her mouth was unbelievably erotic, and her lips parted to let a little sigh of pleasure through. He did it all again, and this time she opened her mouth and gave his finger a teasing nip, which made him laugh. But the laughter faded at once, and he dropped his head to take up the work with the tip of his tongue.

Her breasts began to rise and fall deeply as long, sighing breaths came from her, revealing that his teasing was filling her with delicious tension. Only half-conscious of her own actions, she began to run her hands over his frame, feeling its steel-sprung tautness, the massive strength that reduced hers to nothing but which was leashed back for her sake.

At last he plunged his tongue deep into her mouth and drew her close against him, caressing her with mounting passion. Their first loving had been an introduction, but now they had traveled deep into the realms of intimacy, learning a million things about each other. Already that knowledge was a part of them, in their flesh, in their hearts.

The smell of him was in her nostrils and it was the smell of the good, rich earth, generous and overflowing, giving freely but only in response to love. It was the smell of life itself, wild and untamed, hot, fertile and abundantly satisfying, and she responded to its excitement as she'd never responded to anything before. In his arms her body seemed to throb with the pulse of the world's rhythm.

She could feel the swelling of his manhood against her legs, and the need to enfold him within herself was overpowering. As soon as she parted her legs she felt him seeking her, then driving in slowly, with infinite patience, giving them both time to savor the exquisite delight. She was aflame with pure sensation, lit up inside by a fire that grew higher with every leisurely thrust, until it roared out of control in an explosion of pleasure that illuminated the whole world for a brief moment before dying out, leaving her shattered and blissful.

As they felt their heartbeats slow with the subsiding of the storm, they clung to each other, as if in consolation for the loss of something glorious. Melanie lay in his arms in a state of perfect content, timing her breathing to his, feeling herself about to slip over the edge into satiated sleep.

And then the whole world shuddered.

She opened her eyes abruptly, feeling the vibrations in the air about her, while a deep, angry groan came up from the earth beneath. Vittorio's arms tightened reassuringly around her, while the sound rumbled on until at last it died away into an anguished whisper.

"Vittorio—that noise—those tremors—were they—?"

"Etna," he confirmed. "Don't worry, it's gone now. She often rumbles like that, but it fades. In this part of the world we say the mountain is angry."

She laughed with relief, but he didn't laugh with her. His face was troubled. "You don't mean you believe superstition like that?" she chided him.

"I don't believe in the spirit of the mountain, and yet—" he sighed and sat up, forcing her to sit too "—let's just say it's brought me back to reality."

"What reality?" she said, with the beginning of dread in her heart, for she could see a look of sadness settling on his face.

He sighed. "It's time I was getting you home. By now someone will have found that horse on his own. They'll be searching for you. They mustn't find you in my arms. That would make a scandal for you."

He was already dressing, not looking at her, and suddenly she couldn't bear the way he'd turned away from her. She drew his head around and kissed him tenderly. He took a gentle hold on her shoulders and returned her kiss, but there was something determined in his expression that made her heart sink. "What is it?" she asked. "It was beautiful—wasn't it?"

His eyes were dark and troubled. "More beautiful than anything I have ever known before," he said softly. "But it would have been better not to. I blame myself."

"Don't talk about blame," she said passionately, "as though we'd done something bad. We wanted each other, and we shared something lovely. What can be wrong with that?"

"Not wrong but—there is a distance between us that cannot be so easily bridged, or only for a moment. You are the *padrona* and I—"

"Stop it," she interrupted fiercely. "I forbid you ever to call me that again, do you hear?"

"I hear." He gave a faint smile.

"Have I said something funny?" she demanded.

"Yes, because you contradict yourself. You wish to pretend that you're not my employer, and to make sure that I obey, you forbid me." He took the sting out of the words by softly brushing her hair back from her face. "That is very funny."

"Yes." She sighed. "I'm sorry. I didn't mean to give you orders."

"But you're very used to giving orders," he reminded her, not bitterly, but simply stating a fact. "You're like a queen sometimes, so sure that you will be obeyed. And why not? People who expect to be obeyed usually are."

"I can't help the way I was raised," she pleaded.

His touch on her face contained an echo of the tenderness with which he had held her during the union of their bodies. "Some things weren't meant to be," he said quietly. "What we had was wonderful, but we stole it. You were raised to be a fine lady, and I was raised to be part of the land, and that's a chasm that cannot be crossed."

She almost answered that love could cross it, but he hadn't spoken of love. She didn't know how he felt about her in his heart as opposed to his flesh, and she too was confused. The one thing she saw clearly was that it would be dangerous to argue with him now when he was tense and racked with pride. She sighed and disengaged herself. "If you feel that way, there's nothing more to be said," she agreed bleakly.

As she said the words, a strange thing happened. All her grazes and bruises, which she'd forgotten about in the joy of his embrace, began to hurt again. But the pain in her heart was greater.

When they were both ready, he helped her mount Zeus and walked down the mountainside, leading the horse. Halfway home, they encountered the search party.

At Terrafiore, Annunciata insisted on fetching a doctor and putting her to bed until he came. As she was going upstairs, Melanie saw Vittorio take Zenia's arm and draw her outside, and that was the last she saw of him.

It was still dark when she awoke next morning, having slept only fitfully. She got stiffly out of bed and opened the shutters of a window that looked out over the countryside. Dawn was breaking, casting a soft light where normally there was harsh color and black shadow. She sat there, drinking in the peace that she so badly needed.

Both her heart and mind were in total turmoil. Her flesh still sang to the music of Vittorio's caresses. Their physical discovery of each other had been ecstatic, glorious, fulfilling. It had left her feeling that her body had been loved as no woman's body had ever been before.

But in the cool light of dawn she tried to be rational. She'd been in Sicily only a short time and had become so intoxicated by the country that she was in danger of losing her senses. Vittorio wasn't just a man. He was the embodiment of a land that had turned her inner certainties upside down. She was no longer in control of herself or her own actions, and her independent spirit rebelled.

All her life she'd known who and what she was and where she belonged in the world. Now she was no longer sure of anything except that she was the woman who had come to life in Vittorio's arms. How far away, then, had seemed all she'd been taught about the things to seek in a man: shared background, intellectual interests, compatible temperament, all the things that had brought her to the edge of accepting Harris. How empty and meaningless they'd become as she'd clasped Vittorio to her, gasping with passionate delight as he'd driven vigorously into her willing body, sending tremors of sweet excitement throughout her.

She wondered if Dulcie had ever been torn two ways as she was now. Had she accepted her new self easily, or had it been a struggle?

It was growing lighter every second. Soon Vittorio would arrive. The sight of him would set her heart hammering, and her flesh would quiver in eager expectancy.

And for what? To see him turn away from her again and hear him speak of a chasm that could not be bridged, because he was unwilling to try? If he had his pride, so had she. She must go away for a few days, perhaps to Catania. When she returned, she would be her own mistress again.

All through breakfast she listened for him, but in vain. At last she heard the sound of hoofbeats outside and tensed, promising herself that she would not let her resolve slip. But when the door opened, it was Annunciata who came in, bearing a letter, which she gave to Melanie, saying, "A little boy delivered it."

She tore it open, but her fearful heart warned her of the contents before she read a word.

"I forgot to tell you," he had written, "that I must attend an exhibition of farm equipment in Palermo. I will be away for several days. It is best. Vittorio."

She crumpled the paper in her hand, wanting to cry out with sudden deprivation. She'd planned a separation, but not like this, not to lose him without warning.

She read the letter again. He'd never mentioned an exhibition in Palermo, and she didn't believe it. His true reason was revealed in the three stark words, 'It is best.' Like her, he was wary of the violence of their attraction and had determinedly put a distance between them, forcing his decision on her in a way that made a mockery of his assertion that he was only her servant. She was briefly angry at the way he'd taken charge of the situation.

Then common sense came to her rescue. He'd done the right thing. But she wasn't going to sit here passively waiting for him to return. She called Zenia and told her to pack for a few days away. Zenia looked both miserable and defiant, and Melanie guessed Vittorio had lectured her sternly about the catapult.

Leo drove her into Catania and she booked into the best hotel she could find. There was plenty to see in the city where Bellini had been born, and the magnificent opera house was doing a festival of his operas. She became a determined tourist, seeing everything, trying the local food, exploring the marvelous fashion shops. With her tall, slim figure she fitted almost everything, and she bought garment after garment, telling herself that her resolution to free herself from Vittorio's spell should be marked with a new appearance.

"I'll have it," she heard herself saying yet again, turning in front of the long mirror to see how one more blouse suited her.

"It might have been made for you, *signorina,*" the saleswoman enthused. "Blue is so perfect with your coloring."

But this blue wasn't perfect, Melanie reflected as she removed the blouse. It was peacock blue, and its vividness looked subtly wrong against her fair skin. But it was already being wrapped up, and suddenly it didn't seem worthwhile to change her mind. She was swept by a sense of futility. What was she doing here, buying clothes she didn't want, as if they would cover the emptiness inside her? She'd been gone from Terrafiore only four days, but already it was too much. When the package was ready, she went straight back to her hotel and checked out. By early evening she was home.

The first thing she saw on her arrival was an unfamiliar car. "It belongs to a man who arrived for you," Annunciata told her. "An Englishman."

Before Melanie could ask any questions there was a footstep in the cloisters and a familiar form appeared out of the shadows. "Surprised?" Harris asked, smiling.

"Yes," she said slowly, "surprised—and so glad."

At that moment she felt nothing but pleasure. Just the sight of his solid, genial presence seemed to banish all her doubts and confusion, reassuring her with his familiar smile. He was tall and heavily built, with light brown hair and regular features. Melanie ran to him, taking his hands eagerly in hers and smiling into his face. "How did you get here? Why didn't you let me know? Oh, it's wonderful to see you."

"How could I let you know, when you'd vanished?" he said, laughing. "Are you really glad to see me?"

"Yes—oh, yes!"

"Then give me a proper kiss to prove it," he insisted, drawing her into his arms and placing his lips firmly on hers.

There was no magic in his embrace, but then, there never had been, Melanie realized. Harris's charm lay in other things, things she was just beginning to appreciate properly.

He drew back. "Still glad to see me?" he asked.

"Of course." Perhaps her voice was a little less enthusiastic now, but Harris didn't notice. He looked up at someone who had appeared out of the shadows and stood watching them. "Ah, there you are, Farnese."

At the name Melanie drew in a sharp breath, and for a wild moment she wanted to cry out a protest. Then she turned her head and found herself looking into Vittorio's eyes, that were completely expressionless as he surveyed her in Harris's arms.

Seven

She freed herself quickly, dismayed and embarrassed at what Vittorio had seen and what he would make of it. If only she could read something in his face, but its sculpted beauty was immobile as though carved from marble, and she knew he would give nothing away unless he chose to. "You're back, then," she said, trying to speak steadily.

"I returned yesterday—*padrona*."

"Did you—find anything at the exhibition?"

His lips twisted slightly. "Every new experience is instructive, if one looks at it the right way."

"What exhibition?" Harris demanded.

"Vittorio went to see an exhibition of farm machinery in Palermo," Melanie explained hastily.

"You mean the past few days?" Harris said, frowning. "That's funny. I get information on these exhibitions all over the world in my estate office, but I don't remember hearing about one in Palermo." He shot a suspicious look at Vittorio. "Where was it exactly, and what were the precise dates?" Vittorio remained silent, looking at Harris coldly. "Speak up," Harris ordered. "I want the details."

Vittorio addressed Melanie. "Do you have any fault to find with me, *padrona?*" he asked, emphasizing the *you* very faintly.

"None at all," she said quickly. "Harris, let's go inside. We have a lot to talk about." She turned to speak to Vittorio, but he had walked away.

"Damned cheek!" Harris exclaimed. "It's all the same with these foreigners. Give them an inch and they take an ell."

"Come inside," she urged again, taking his arm and almost dragging him away. Inside the house she faced him. "You shouldn't have spoken to him like that."

"In heaven's name, why not?"

"Because for one thing, you have no authority to question Vittorio's actions. If *I'm* satisfied, that's the end of it."

"And you're 'satisfied' with a flimsy story like that? Come on, darling. It was a try-on. There was no exhibition, and it didn't do any harm to let him know that I'd seen through his tricks."

"Harris, please stop this," she said desperately.

At once he was solicitous. "Darling, I didn't mean to upset you."

"I'm not upset," she said quickly. "It's just that Vittorio is vital to Terrafiore. He practically *is* Terrafiore—"

"And he's made you afraid of offending him. Very clever. I wonder what other tricks he's up to. Creaming off a percentage, I shouldn't wonder. I know the type. You have to be firm with them."

If he said any more she would scream. One picture haunted her mind—Vittorio's carefully blank face as he saw her kissing Harris. How long had he been there? Long enough to see the moment of gladness that had taken her into Harris's arms, a moment she was now regretting?

"Of course he isn't creaming off a percentage," she said angrily. "You know nothing about him."

"All right, I'll say no more," he soothed. "I'm here to shoulder your troubles, not add to them."

"When did you get here?"

"Just a few hours ago. I hired the car at the airport and drove up here. I must admit I got lost a few times but I made it in the end. I shan't be sorry to get back to civilization, though."

Her temper, which seemed to be permanently on edge these days, flared up. "It might interest you to know that Sicily has been invaded by some of the most cultured peoples the world has ever seen, and they've all left their mark. They'd probably have called us uncivilized. Didn't you see the mosaics outside?"

"Oh sure, that artsy stuff is all very well," Harris said easily. "You know it doesn't mean anything to me. I'm talking about real civilization. You know, water coming out of taps and things happening when you touch switches."

"We have all the comforts, including electricity from our own generator and water from our own well."

"Hey, hey, all right. Don't eat me."

"I don't like you bad-mouthing my home just because it isn't like England," she said firmly.

"Your home?" he echoed blankly. The words seemed to make him look at her properly for the first time. "It's just as well I came," he mused. "You're looking thin and tired, like she said."

"Just as who said?"

"Your friend—the one who called me. She said you seemed ill and you'd been acting oddly. And there was something about a runaway horse, but I couldn't follow the details. Her English wasn't too good."

"Did she give a name?"

"No, just said she was a friend of yours, and I ought to come out quickly."

Melanie stared. "But I haven't mentioned you to anyone. There's nobody who *could* have called you."

"Well, somebody did."

Melanie frowned. "I wonder if it could have been Salvani's wife, Irena. The lawyer had your number. She might have got it from him. Perhaps she thought you'd persuade me to sell."

"I'm surprised you need any persuading."

"That's because you haven't seen how beautiful Terrafiore is," Melanie said earnestly.

He smiled and took hold of her shoulders. "I remember when you used to think Brackenhurst was beautiful," he said, naming his own estate. "You had such plans for it. You'd even designed the outhouse I'm going to build for your kiln so that you can go on with your pottery business. Have you forgotten all that?"

She *had* forgotten it, but his words brought everything back in a rush, the estate workers, many of them old friends, all expecting her to become Lady Brennan, Harris's beautiful old house with the dogs that swarmed riotously around her whenever she went there, his mother who treated her as a daughter, all the things she'd loved and cherished. A sudden wave of homesickness washed over her.

"How are things at home?" she asked with a slight huskiness in her voice.

"Let's have dinner, and you can hear all about it," he promised. "Come up and let me show you the room Annunciata has given me."

"No," she said quickly, "I have something to do first. You go up and get ready."

When she'd seen him climb the stairs, she slipped out of the house and went to look for Vittorio. But Leo told her he'd just left to inspect the vineyards and wouldn't be back that day. "Tell him—ask him to see me first thing tomorrow," she instructed Leo, and went in to dress for dinner.

She dressed in an elegant blue silk that she knew Harris liked, and began to go through the drawers of her dressing table, looking for the earrings that would go with it. Then she stopped, puzzled.

Before leaving England she'd slipped a snapshot of Harris into her purse. At Terrafiore she'd put the picture into a dressing table drawer, carefully enclosed between the pages of her address book. They were still there, but the picture had been removed and now lay on its own, while the address book was open at the page with Harris's telephone number. It was as though someone had gone through her things and neglected to replace them properly, but surely only Zenia came into this room?

And then Melanie knew who had called Harris.

"She wouldn't dare," she said aloud, but even as she said it she knew that Zenia would dare anything, because she was in love and love knew no rules. To keep Vittorio to herself, she would go through Melanie's possessions, searching for something she could use. The picture with its inscription, *Hurry back to me—Harris,* would give her the idea, and then she must have hunted through the address book until she found the number. It was a risk, but Zenia was desperate.

She found her earrings and went downstairs, still thoughtful. Harris was waiting for her at the bottom step, smiling and holding out a bouquet. "Flowers for my lady," he said with a flourish. "Admittedly I took them from your own garden, which spoils it a bit, but the thought is there."

She laughed and accepted them. Zenia was just coming in, so Melanie gave her the flowers and told her to put them in water, noticing the quick, questioning glance Zenia gave her and Harris, which confirmed her suspicions.

He might consider himself in the wilds, but Harris's code demanded that he dress impeccably for the occasion, so he'd put on a dinner jacket and black bow tie. He led her to the table and held the chair out for her with old-fashioned courtesy, then took his own seat at a right angle and squeezed her hand.

Zenia served the meal and Melanie knew a moment's intense pride when Harris tried it. "This is really good," he exclaimed over the pasta with aubergine.

"Not so uncivilized as all that?" Melanie teased him, and they laughed together.

"It's good to see you again, darling," he said warmly. "I've missed you so much. I didn't think you'd be away this long. I want to hear everything that's happened. Have you met Salvani yet?"

"Have I ever!" she exclaimed grimly, and gave him an account of how Salvani had stopped her on the road from the airport, and what had happened after the dinner party.

"Good grief! You mean he tried to—?"

"I don't know what he'd have done if Vittorio hadn't arrived. Perhaps he just meant to keep me there until he'd forced a signature out of me. But that's the kind of man he is, and I don't see why I should tamely give in and sell to him."

"Well, I dare say we could find another buyer. I'm surprised to see you so contented out here, knowing you like the bright lights."

"Do I? Yes, I suppose I do," she mused. The truth was that since she'd arrived, she hadn't given a thought to her crowded social life in England.

"And this house. Of course it's beautiful, but it's vast and empty. Does Dulcie's ghost haunt you?"

He laughed at his own joke, but Melanie stared at him. "Do you know," she said slowly, "in a strange way that's exactly what's happened. I've come to understand her more since I've seen Terrafiore. I know now why she loved—Sicily, and why she couldn't tear herself away."

"Well, I hope you're going to tear yourself away soon," he said, seeming not to notice her stumble. "You've seen what you wanted to see. What is there to keep you?"

She didn't answer, because she couldn't. How could she tell Harris that the thought of never seeing Vittorio again hurt her almost physically? But neither was she ready to turn her back on her own country forever. "Tell me what's been happening at home?" she said hastily. "Has Sal had her pups yet?"

"Last week, three boys and four girls. I've picked out the prettiest little bitch for you. You'll love her. Your father's cook made me bring you some of her homemade chutney because she's sure 'them foreigners' aren't feeding you properly. And Mother's roses took first prize at the agricultural show just after you left. I promised her I'd show you the clipping from the local paper."

He took it out of his pocket, and Melanie studied the picture of Lady Brennan with her trophy. Harris embarked on a funny story about a dispute between two of their grumpy neighbors. He told it well, and Melanie laughed out loud, feeling again a touch of nostalgia for the old happy life with its certainties and contentment.

She'd seen Harris's least attractive side that afternoon. As if to make up for it, he now showed himself at his best, evoking all the memories they'd shared over their years of growing up together, subtly reminding her of everything she was missing. After the stress of the past few days, this restful evening was balm to her troubled spirit, and she found that she was enjoying herself. When dinner was over, they relaxed on the sofa with brandies and black coffee, talking and laughing, and it was nearly one in the morning when they climbed the stairs.

"Good night, Harris," she said sleepily.

He planted a light kiss on her lips. "Good night, darling." He looked at her quizzically. "Are you glad I came?"

She nodded. "I needed to get my sense of proportion back."

He smiled and went down the corridor to his own room.

She slept longer than usual the following morning and awoke to find the sun high in the sky. She hurried down and found Harris waiting for her in the kitchen, sipping a cup of coffee.

"At last, sleepyhead," he chided her with a grin.

"I'm three hours later than usual," she exclaimed. "Why didn't they wake me?"

"I told them not to," he admitted. "You looked so worn out when I first saw you yesterday that I was shocked. You needed that extra sleep."

Her look of weariness was because of mental conflict over Vittorio, but she couldn't say that, so she just smiled and poured herself some coffee. "I think I'll skip breakfast," she said. "I must go and find Vittorio. He always explains to me what his plan for the day is."

"Surely as his employer it should be for you to tell him?" Harris said.

"How can I when he knows about Terrafiore and I don't?"

Harris nodded. "That's what he wants you to think. It's as well that I came. You won't be troubled by him anymore. I've arranged everything."

Melanie stared at him. "What on earth do you mean?"

"I've dismissed him."

"You've *what?*"

"When he showed up this morning I told him you no longer required his services. It was the only thing to do, darling. I could see he'd practically got you hypnotized into thinking he was essential to Terrafiore. So you were afraid to put him in his place, and frankly he was presuming. Well, I made it clear that he'd have me to deal with if he gave any more trouble."

"You—to deal with?" she echoed slowly. "You think you frightened him, do you?"

"Let's say he recognized the voice of authority."

If she hadn't been so angry, she could have laughed at the picture of the powerful, intensely masculine Vittorio being cowed by Harris. She stared at him, feeling the fragile mood of the evening before crack and fall to pieces about her, leaving only disgust and indignation that spilled out in the furious epithet, "You *clown*, Harris!"

"Eh—what did you call me?"

"I called you a clown, and so you are. How dare you interfere with something you know nothing about! And how dare you talk about me as though I'm a silly little thing who swoons the first time a man flexes his muscles! You should know me better. Vittorio hasn't hypnotized me. He *is* essential to Terrafiore. Who's going to run it without him? You?"

"It hadn't occurred to me, but I manage a pretty big estate at home. And one is pretty much like another, I suppose."

"Then you suppose wrong," she stormed. "And you were never more wrong than when you presumed to dismiss my staff without reference to me."

She turned and ran out of the house, calling to Leo to saddle Rosa for her. Harris trotted after her, making ineffectual remonstrances. "Stay out of my way, Harris," she snapped as she swung herself up onto the mare's back.

"But where do you think you're going?" he protested.

"To see Vittorio and try to undo some of the damage you've done."

"You won't go to that oaf's place alone, surely?"

She swung Rosa around, and in another moment she was out of the yard and galloping up the slope. Her heart was suddenly filled with a terrible dread. Suppose Vittorio should have decided to cut his losses forever and just go? Suppose she found the cottage empty and no sign of him? She urged Rosa on.

At last the little stone building came into sight. To her fearful eyes there was something bleak and dead about it.

The door was closed and the shutters drawn, and there was no sign of Vittorio. She hurried the last few yards, trying not to think of the void there would be in her life if Vittorio had disappeared. At the foot of the little path, she jumped down and tethered Rosa, running up to his closed front door, hammering on it.

But then she saw the black stallion in the distance and Vittorio on his back, riding like a madman, his hair whipped behind him in rhythm with the horse's mane. As before, Melanie had the sense that they were one creature, a beautiful, wild creature that would never be broken by force but could be tamed by love. She ran down the path to where the land flattened out and watched them in ecstasy.

Vittorio saw her and instantly came closer, but instead of halting he wheeled back, circling her, still galloping at top speed. She turned to watch him, around and around, turning until she was dizzy, while he circled endlessly, as though he were binding her with invisible ropes. *"Vittorio,"* she cried.

He slowed to a halt and sat looking at her broodingly from a few yards away. She had a sharp sense of the indecision that racked him. Part of him wanted to come to her, part of him was on the brink of heading over the hills on the stallion's back and never returning. "Vittorio," she said again, pleading.

He jumped down, took off the rope halter and slapped the horse on the rump. When it had gone, he faced her, scowling.

"I wish you'd taken me up on him again," she said impulsively.

He gave a crack of mirthless laughter. "Why don't you get the Englishman to catch and break him for you?"

"I don't want to own him. That would be to change him, and he's perfect as he is."

"And besides, the Englishman couldn't do it," Vittorio jeered.

"He's not a Sicilian," Melanie agreed, and saw Vittorio's lip curl in ironic appreciation of this touch. But the anger still sparkled from his eyes. "I'm sorry about what happened. I've only just found out. Harris had no power to dismiss you."

Vittorio shrugged. "You—him, what difference does it make?"

"But I never meant to fire you."

"No? Wasn't that why you sent me a message to report to you this morning?"

"I *asked* you to see me so that I could apologize for Harris's behavior last night," she said passionately.

"Ah, yes, the aristocracy have such fine manners, haven't they? Apologize one moment and stab you in the back the next."

"I told you, I never meant to fire you," she repeated.

He shrugged again and made his way up the path. Melanie followed him into the cottage. "You'll come back now, won't you?" she pleaded.

"No, I can't do that," he said, not looking at her.

"But why?"

He turned suddenly, his eyes flashing scorn. "Because you were not honest with me," he said bitterly.

"I don't know what you mean. How was I not honest with you?"

"You should have told me you were another man's woman."

"But I— Vittorio, what did Harris say to you?"

"Enough."

"No, I won't be put off like that," she cried. "What did he say?"

"That you are his promised wife."

She drew a sharp breath. "That isn't true. I've never promised to marry him. Do you think, if I were his fiancée, that you and I—?" She stopped, assailed by dizzying memories of his arms and the heat of his body.

"How do I know what you'd do?" he demanded coldly. "I don't know what fine English ladies think right. Perhaps to *Lady* Melanie Carlyle it seems natural to amuse herself with a servant before she marries a man of her own kind."

"That's a wicked thing to say," she cried furiously. "And why must you always talk of yourself as a servant?"

"Because it's what I am," he flung at her. "I'm your hired man. I live on your land, by your favor. You can walk into my house whenever you choose, but I must wait for permission to enter yours. I take your money in wages and you can dismiss me when I'm no longer required. What am I but a servant?"

"Oh, God," she whispered, rent by the unconsciously revealed agony in his voice.

"But you must admit I serve you well," he went on with cold savagery.

"No one could run Terrafiore better, but—"

"That's not what I meant. I serve you well in other ways, don't I?"

The bitter emphasis on "serve" brought home to her suddenly the way he was using the word, and she flushed with anger. Her temper rose, she lashed out blindly and would have struck his cheek if he hadn't caught her wrist. "Now we have the truth," he said grimly. "This is what you really came for, isn't it? You wanted to enjoy yourself one last time with your rough lover before you marry that Englishman with the woman's hands and the pale skin. Well, why not? You've paid me up to the end of the week.''

Before she could protest, he pulled her against him and covered her mouth fiercely with his own. It was a hard, bruising kiss, a demonstration of sheer power, devoid of tenderness. Through it she could feel his anger and bitterness, his humiliated pride and his arrogant conviction of superiority. All this ran through her like lightning, and at the same time the true meaning of his last words came to her, inflaming her rage. She tried to push him away, but his arms were like steel hawsers around her, imprisoning her while his lips ravaged hers.

''You should have told me what you really wanted of me,'' he grated. ''Then I could have earned my keep properly.''

''Vittorio, no—'' she managed to gasp. ''Not like this—please. You'll hate both me and yourself afterward.''

''I couldn't hate myself more than I already do,'' he growled savagely.

''And me?'' she panted. ''Do you hate me?''

''Haven't I reason?'' he whispered as his mouth crushed hers again. She felt his tongue forcing its way between her lips, flickering hard over the soft inner surface of her mouth. Against her will, the familiar fire came to life, streaming along her nerves until it flamed over her body, making every inch of her throb with desire. It would be so easy to yield to his demanding passion, but she fought down her sensations, knowing that what was between them must be more than physical delight, or it was nothing. Whatever happened, she would never make love with him this way, for the shame and bitterness that would be left behind would poison their relationship forever.

She pressed her hands against him, trying to ignore the treacherous delight at the awareness of his powerful frame next to hers, his hand pressing into the small of her back, grinding her against him so that she was intimately conscious of his flesh and the way it was responding to her. She could feel his manhood, hard and urgent, eager for their union, just as she was secretly eager for it. Her mind was filled with thoughts and pictures of passion, memories of how they had been together, how they could be again, but she fought them back and twisted violently away from him. "For pity's sake, stop this," she said fiercely. "You don't really mean it. You've gone mad."

Suddenly he became very still. She could hear his harsh breathing close to her ear, but he was motionless, and gradually she felt the tension drain out of him. She exerted all her strength to escape, and his arms fell away from her so easily that she staggered. Vittorio didn't put out a hand to steady her. He seemed almost afraid to touch her. His eyes were full of horror. "My God!" he whispered, appalled. "What was I doing?"

He turned away from her and ran shaking hands through his hair. "Mad," he said in a strained voice. "You're right—mad, with a madness I can't control."

He turned back to her. "Why don't you run from me while you can?" he demanded harshly.

She faced him. "Why? Should I be afraid of you?"

He shook his head. "No—I could never harm you. It's just that for a moment—the thought of you with another man—" His eyes were terrible. "Why did you have to come here now?" he groaned.

"Don't you understand why?" she asked softly. "I came because I couldn't do anything else. I ran away from you because I wanted to break what's between us. I was afraid of it." She looked into his face as she said this, and he nodded, silently telling her that his feelings mirrored hers. "But I had to come back and find you."

"And instead you found the Englishman and ran into his arms," he said sardonically.

She remembered Vittorio's cool, blank eyes as he'd watched her in Harris's embrace. Now she was seeing the pain that lay behind the mask, and it invaded her heart, becoming her pain, too. She tried to protest, but he silenced her with a gesture.

"Listen to me. Last night I came back to the house when it was dark. I stood outside and looked in at you and him, sitting at the dinner table. Your hand was in his, and you were smiling at him." He closed his eyes, as if trying to shut out the sight.

"That didn't mean anything," Melanie insisted. "He was just telling me about people at home, and it was pleasant, but that's all."

"That's not what *I* saw. I saw a man and woman who were a couple. Can you look me in the eyes and tell me that wasn't how you felt at that moment—that he was the man you should be with?"

"Maybe I did. I don't know. Vittorio, try and understand. I'd been so confused and troubled, and I grew up with Harris. It was a relief to see him and—yes, I was glad, but only because he made me feel comfortable. Why is it so important?"

"Because that's why I accepted my dismissal from him, why I believed him when he said you were his fiancée— because seeing you with him had made me understand what a fool I'd been to dream that—'' He checked himself.

"Yes?" Melanie breathed. "What had you dreamed?"

"It doesn't matter now," he said harshly. "I had foolish hopes—the kind a clown has, hopes that can't survive the light of reality. I fled, just as you did, but I found myself coming back because I have to be where you are. But *he* was there, and you ran into his arms, and I understood that I'd been your plaything."

"Vittorio, I swear to you that's not true."

"Perhaps it's better for you if it is true," he said somberly. "Go back to him."

"I can't go away and leave you like this."

"You need not worry. I'll return to run Terrafiore. I won't leave you stranded in his ignorant hands." His lip curled derisively. "So you see, you've gained what you came for. Now, please leave."

She was about to refuse when she remembered his bitter words. "You can walk into my house whenever you choose." To stay against his will would be to deny him his dignity. She turned and walked out into the harsh sunlight. A moment later she'd mounted Rosa and galloped off. She didn't look back, or she might have seen him at the window, not moving until she'd vanished from sight.

Eight

Harris was absent when she arrived back at the villa, but he returned after an hour. He was smiling as he said, "Now I understand what's really going on."

"What does that mean?"

"I've been to see Salvani. I wanted to speak to him about what you told me."

"I suppose he had a plausible explanation?"

"Well, honestly, darling, I can't help feeling you got it a bit wrong. His account makes much more sense. He stopped to talk and you panicked. He's very apologetic and so I said I was sure you were sorry for your behavior, too."

"*What?*"

"You were overwrought, of course, but I think you went a bit far with your nail scissors. Actually threatening to put out his eyes—well!"

"Was Irena there?" Melanie demanded wryly.

"Yes, and that's another thing that convinces me you misunderstood. He described everything to his wife so frankly—"

"After the state he was in when he went home, he wouldn't have much choice."

"You mean after Farnese knocked him about?" Harris asked grimly.

"After Vittorio saved me from him, and then got beaten up for his pains," she said emphatically. Harris's expression was cynical, and it goaded Melanie to add. "Did Salvani happen to mention that he deliberately sabotaged me in the procession?"

"He told me you didn't manage your horse very well because of the sidesaddle, and there was a certain amount of amusement. I should think that alone would make you want to come home. How you can stay here with a crowd of yokels who've seen you looking a fool, I can't imagine."

"But don't you see, that's why he did it, to drive me away? It wasn't an accident. That was a circus horse and the band played the right tunes because Salvani told them to."

Harris looked at her in kindly amusement. "Do you have the slightest proof of that mad suggestion?"

"I saw him talking to the band leader before we started."

"And heard what they were saying?"

"No, but—"

"I thought not. It's all crazy fantasy without a shred of evidence. I think the sun must have got to you. Or should I say Farnese got to you, with his version of events? I've heard about his grandiose ideas of being the true heir to Terrafiore."

"He *is* the true heir," Melanie insisted. She snatched up the picture of Giorgio and held it out. "Can't you see the resemblance?"

"No, I can't," Harris said after a brief glance. "Anyway, if Giorgio was his father, why didn't he leave him a share in this place?"

Melanie sighed. "I don't know."

"But I do. Farnese has no rights here, and he knows it. There's no resemblance, darling." He smiled and tried to take her hands. "When I think that you've always been so sensible..."

Melanie moved quickly away from him. "All the things I've thought of as sensible don't seem so sensible anymore."

"Well, at least you realize that you're losing your sense of proportion."

She turned on him angrily. "What about *your* sense of proportion? You're so determined to make me sell that you take Salvani's view of everything, without considering the other side."

"Or perhaps I'm better at assessing another man than a woman who's had her wits addled by—well, let's say by the sun," Harris retorted. "I was impressed by Salvani. He's a solid man, a man of substance. In a foreign sort of way, he's one of our own kind."

One of our own kind. She'd heard the phrase often before in the comfortable well-bred community where she'd been raised. Suddenly it sounded sinister. "That's nonsense," she said shortly.

"I think it makes sense. I did the right thing in getting rid of Farnese."

"He's coming back," Melanie said firmly.

Harris turned abruptly and stared at her. "*What?* You actually allowed him back here? I don't believe it."

"Well, start believing it. And I didn't allow him back, I *begged* him to come back, because Terrafiore needs him. What's more, I told him I hadn't promised to marry you."

"Well, of all the— do you realize you've made a fool of me—undermined my authority—?"

"You have no authority on Terrafiore. I wish you'd realize that."

"Well, thank you very much for your loyalty," he said angrily.

"Loyalty!" she cried. "Do you call it loyal to take Salvani's side against me?"

"I call it sensible to consider the facts." Harris's lips tightened in the cold anger that was the nearest he came to temper. "I think we'd better say no more for the moment. We'll talk later, when we're both in a more suitable frame of mind."

"Certainly," she snapped, and watched, seething, as he walked out into the yard. She was hurt and taken aback by his behavior. It had never occurred to her that he'd find excuses for Salvani, but her enemy's explanation was so horribly plausible, and it seemed that Harris had chosen to believe what suited him.

She went upstairs to her room and opened the door so quickly that the person inside was taken by surprise and had no time to stop what she was doing. For a moment Melanie and Zenia stood petrified, staring at each other, both equally taken aback.

The wardrobe was open and several garments were strewn on the bed. Zenia was standing in front of the long mirror, holding the peacock-blue blouse against her, and it was obvious that she'd been spending a blissful hour going through Melanie's clothes. She whirled when she heard the door open, still clutching the blouse, and in that moment Melanie understood why the lovely garment had seemed subtly wrong against her delicate English fairness. The deep, glowing color demanded a woman whose coloring was equally rich and overpowering, a woman with southern beauty, warm skin and an exotic presence. In fact, it demanded Zenia.

Melanie closed the door and came into the room. Zenia stayed as she was, her head held defiantly high, evidently too proud to scuttle about trying to hide what she was doing. With her long black hair and flashing eyes, she looked magnificent, Melanie thought.

After a moment of resounding silence, Zenia tossed her hair and said haughtily, "So now you're going to dismiss me. I don't care. I leave your house at once."

"Stop talking like a heroine in a melodrama," Melanie commanded. "Of course I'm not going to dismiss you. It wasn't very polite to try my clothes without asking me, but I can understand the temptation, especially when a woman looks like you."

Zenia's dramatic pose collapsed like a house of cards, leaving an eager, frustrated girl. "Sometimes I think I would gladly die to have some beautiful things," she said passionately. "I see wealthy tourists come to Sicily. They load themselves with jewels and expensive clothes, and they look like donkeys with bells on. Me, I have no money, but I have style, I know I have."

"Yes," agreed Melanie, "you have style. And it's natural. You're very lucky."

Zenia gave a little wistful sigh. "Am I?"

"Put this on," Melanie said, indicating the blouse. When Zenia looked doubtful, she said. "Go on."

Zenia pulled off her shabby top and slipped on the peacock blouse. It looked superb against her warm skin. She turned this way and that, looking at herself in the mirror, smiling with pleasure. For a moment her hostility to Melanie was forgotten.

"You can have it," Melanie said.

Zenia stared. "You don't mean that."

"Of course I mean it. I can never wear it again."

Zenia's face hardened again. "You mean you can't wear it after *I've* worn it?" she snapped.

Melanie sighed. "Will you stop being so prickly? I only meant that it suits you better than me. If I wore it now, I should always be horribly conscious that it didn't look right on me. Please, I want you to have it."

She could see the struggle written on the young woman's face, but the result was a foregone conclusion. No power on earth could have made Zenia refuse the blouse that emphasized her beauty so dramatically.

"Thank you," she said with sudden shyness. She removed the blouse and put on her old one, folding her new possession away with loving care.

Melanie watched her, and kindly interest prompted her to ask. "Why do you stay here, Zenia? If you went to Rome or Milan you could make a career as a model."

"Oh, I would like that so much." Zenia sighed. "I dream of going somewhere where there are lights and excitement, and lovely clothes, and I wouldn't have to wash the dishes. Every day I mean to go, but—but I can't tear myself away from here."

Melanie nodded. It would break Zenia's heart to go where she wouldn't see Vittorio anymore. "I understand," she said sympathetically.

But it was the wrong thing to say. Zenia looked at her suspiciously and her face hardened. "You'd like me to go, wouldn't you?" she snapped. "You'd like to be rid of me because..."

She broke off with a sob and ran from the room, but she remembered to snatch up the blouse before she went.

Harris was in a better mood over lunch. He might almost have forgotten their row of the morning, except that his speech was a little more clipped than usual. "Why don't we go out this afternoon?" he suggested. "You can show me around."

Melanie agreed willingly. Despite everything, the habit of liking and trusting Harris was still strong, and she clung to the hope that once he saw how beautiful Terrafiore was he would be more willing to see things from her point of view.

She slipped out ahead of him and went to find Leo to tell him to put her normal saddle onto Zeus. Harris fancied himself as a devil on horseback, able to master the most recalcitrant beast. The truth was that he had a poor seat and heavy hands, so Melanie quietly arranged for him to ride the placid Rosa. There was no sign of Vittorio, but Leo volunteered the information that he'd arrived, given orders and gone again.

She showed Harris the fields and orchards that Vittorio had shown her on the first day, trying to convey to him some of the enthusiasm that she'd learned to feel for the beautiful land, but she knew she wasn't getting through to him.

"It's an impressive place," Harris finally agreed, mopping his brow. "Is there much more of it?"

"A very great deal more. Vittorio says I still haven't seen most of it. But what do you think? Isn't it glorious?"

He grunted. "It's probably worth a good bit."

"Is that all you can find to say about it?" she asked exasperated.

"I'm thinking of your welfare. You're entitled to a decent price. It may even be worth more than Salvani's offering."

"Almost certainly, I should think. After what he's done so far, I'm sure he's trying to cheat me on the price, too. I expect that's why he wants a quick sale, before I've had time to find out its true value."

Harris sighed. "You really have got your knife into Salvani."

Melanie didn't answer, because her attention had been taken by something in the distance. Her heart leaped as she saw Vittorio astride the black stallion, riding him bareback, with the rope halter.

Vittorio drew up close to them. Harris's lips tightened and he greeted Vittorio with a curt nod. Vittorio returned it before addressing Melanie. "I've been making a final check over the fields," he said. "Everything is ready for the harvest."

"Does that mean you'll be engaging casual labor?" she asked.

"I've already done that."

"Without her ladyship's prior approval?" Harris demanded, frowning.

Vittorio looked at him with pity. "If I'd waited for that, the best laborers would have been engaged by other farmers long ago."

"You did the right thing," Melanie said quickly.

But Harris couldn't let well alone. "I think you should know," he said to Vittorio, "that I've been to see Signor Salvani."

If this was meant to abash Vittorio it failed. There was a look of contempt on his face as he said, "I've no doubt that you got in to see him easily. That's more than I can do."

"Is there any reason why he should wish to see you?" Harris demanded, a touch haughtily.

Vittorio smiled unpleasantly. "On the contrary, *signore,* after what happened in the procession, he has every reason not to want to see me. He values his skin too much." Abruptly Vittorio switched his attention to Melanie. "I hope your injuries are healed now."

"I'm fine now, but let Salvani alone. I don't want him setting anyone else on you." To forestall further argument, she put out a hand to the stallion and was delighted when he didn't flinch away. "I'm glad he came back to you."

"I was in the Jeep and he suddenly appeared a few minutes ago," Vittorio said.

Harris was looking closely at the stallion. "That looks like a valuable animal," he observed. He shot a suspicious look at Vittorio. "Who does he belong to?"

"To no one," Vittorio informed him. "He is wild."

"He looks tame enough to me," Harris observed.

Vittorio's gaze was bland and innocent. "Perhaps you would like to try him, *signore?*"

"No," Melanie said at once, appalled by the vision this conjured up.

"Why ever not?" Harris demanded.

"Because it's getting late and the heat is giving me a headache, and I'd like to be turning back," she improvised hastily. She frowned at Vittorio and turned away. Harris followed her reluctantly. Melanie glanced over her shoulder at Vittorio and saw him looking at Harris with a derisive grin on his face.

Vittorio stayed close behind them for a mile, until they came to the place where he'd parked the Jeep. Then he dismounted, freed the stallion and got into the vehicle. A minute later, he passed them on the road and roared into the distance. When they arrived back at the house, the Jeep was standing in the yard. Melanie dismounted, tossed her rein to Leo and went looking for Vittorio. She found him in the stable. "Why did you take his side?" he demanded sardonically.

"I had to. Harris couldn't have ridden that stallion."

He gave a mirthless laugh. "I know. I saw the way he was riding."

"You were deliberately trying to make a fool of him."

"Just as he tried to make a fool of me. But he was lucky. He had you to protect him." Vittorio's mouth curled with contempt as he said "protect." "Perhaps next time he won't be able to hide behind you."

"There isn't going to be a next time," she said firmly. "I forbid it."

"Because you're afraid for him? You should be. If he were a man of my race, I'd give him a knife and take one myself, and we'd see who was the better man."

"But he isn't of your race," she flashed, alarmed at a fierce light that burned in Vittorio's eyes.

"No, he is of *your* race, so he feels no shame in accepting your protection—or rather, he wouldn't feel any if he had the wit to realize you *were* protecting him. You needn't worry. I won't harm him unless—" He broke off, his eyes glittering.

"Unless?" Melanie echoed, half-hypnotized.

"Unless he tries to harm Terrafiore. Then let him look over his shoulder with every step he takes, for I shall be there."

Before she could reply, a shadow in the doorway warned her that Leo was approaching with the horses. She dropped her voice to say, "It's difficult enough having Harris here. Don't make it worse."

She walked quickly away and hurried up to her room, longing for a cool shower. She reached up to untie the silk scarf she'd been wearing about her neck, then remembered that she'd taken it off and tied it to her saddle. She made a sound of annoyance with herself and went down again to retrieve it. The stables were silent as she approached, and for a moment she thought no one was there. But in the doorway she stopped.

Vittorio was standing deep in the shadows, with her scarf in his hand. He didn't see her, and she watched, holding her breath, as he raised it slowly, inhaling the odor of her perfume, his eyes closed. Then he dropped his head suddenly, hiding his face in the delicate silk as he had once hidden it against her silky skin in an ecstasy of passion.

Suddenly a shudder seemed to go through his tense body. With an angry gesture he threw the scarf to the ground and now Melanie could see that his face was hard with rejection. But the moment passed almost at once, and the next instant he stopped to seize up the scarf again, thrusting it quickly into his pocket.

"Vittorio..." Melanie didn't even know she'd spoken until his name emerged from her lips. He looked up quickly.

"Why do you spy on me?" he demanded harshly.

She came deeper into the stable and stood close to him. "I didn't mean to spy on you. But I'm glad I came when I did. Now I know something you wouldn't have told me."

"Does it please you to know that I'm still your fool, despite myself?"

"Yes, because I'm a fool, too."

He grimaced. "Pretty words, but they mean nothing. Why don't you go back to England and marry that milksop? I thought you were good for Terrafiore. I thought I could teach you the wisdom of the earth because you were willing to learn. Now I wonder.''

An ache of disappointment washed over her, for these weren't the words she wanted to hear. "Is that all you care about?" she demanded angrily. "That I should be good for the land?"

In the dim light of the stable she saw the glitter of his eyes as he returned, "What else is there?"

"Us," she said passionately.

"There is no 'us.' There never can be."

"There is," she flung at him. "There has to be. You want it, too. Don't deny it."

"I don't deny it, but a man doesn't have to take what he wants."

"But he does," she said. "We've tried to run away from each other and it doesn't work."

He turned haggard, angry eyes on her. "And how do I know you won't go again?"

"Because of this," she said softly, putting her hands behind his head and drawing it down until she could lay her lips against his. At first she thought he was going to resist her, but after a moment of tension the rigidity left his body. She worked on him with all the skill and sub-tlety at her command, using her lips to remind him of the very things he was trying to forget, weaving spells about him.

"Melanie..." he groaned, "don't do this...."

"Why not, if I want to?" she whispered. "Let's be fools together."

"There's a penalty for folly," he said against her lips as his arms went around her.

"Then we'll pay it together, and it'll be worth it."

"Yes," he said hoarsely, "it'll be worth it."

On the words, he crushed her mouth with his own, kissing her like a man possessed, winding his fingers through her hair. Melanie closed her eyes and gave herself up ecstatically to the kiss, thinking that if only they were in his cottage, safe from prying eyes—

A noise made her open her eyes reluctantly, just in time to see someone moving quickly away from the door. She couldn't make out who it was, but from his height she had a suspicion that it had been Harris.

"What is it?" Vittorio growled as he felt her stiffen.

"I think Harris saw us."

"Good. Then he knows now that you belong to me and not to him," Vittorio said grimly. "It was time he knew. Shall I tell him for you in words?"

"No, thank you," she said hastily. "I can do that. And no knives, for pity's sake."

He held up his hands, as if placating her. "For you, I'm a pussycat. You deal with him as you like." But as he was heading out of the door, he stopped and turned back to her, "Just the same, I think it's best if he doesn't stay too long."

At dinner that evening, Melanie waited for Harris to bring up the subject, but he seemed determined not to. He praised Annunciata for the food but without producing a softening of her expression, and then turned the conversation to the black stallion. "Do you know what a beast like that would be worth, properly broken?" he asked. "I reckon—"

"Harris, please leave that subject for the moment," Melanie said desperately. "There's something we have to talk about."

"Is there?" he said coolly. "I would have thought least said, soonest mended."

"It was you in the stable this afternoon, wasn't it?"

"Of course it was. I can't say I'm surprised. I'd begun to suspect something of the kind."

"I'm sorry you had to find out like that—"

"Darling, listen, don't get het up about this. Let's keep it in perspective. I'm a man of the world. I know what hot sun and a different setting can do. The natives look beautiful and—well, one lets one's hair down. Enjoy your little holiday romance. It has nothing to do with you and me."

She looked at him curiously. "You're not jealous?"

"Naturally," Harris said heartily, although his face showed no disturbance. "But it can't be serious. I know you too well to think you'd give up reality for a pretty shadow."

"Do you, Harris? Do you really think you know me well?"

"I've known you all your life."

"So have I. But I'm beginning to think *I* don't know me at all."

For the past few seconds, she'd been vaguely aware of a noise outside that sounded like someone arriving in a car. Now Annunciata hurried in, looking anxious. "Signor Salvani is here," she said.

"Salvani?" Melanie echoed indignantly. "He's got a nerve showing his face here."

"Actually, I invited him," Harris admitted.

"You did what?"

"I thought if you two got together we could sort out the misunderstanding."

"There's no misunderstanding. I don't want him here, as you know perfectly well, or you'd have told me."

"I didn't tell you because I was afraid you'd react like this. Believe me, Melanie, it really is better for us all to sit down and discuss things like rational beings."

Before she could say any more, the bulky frame of Salvani appeared in the doorway, smiling all over his pasty face. He advanced on Melanie with his arms outstretched. "This is good," he declared. "This is how it should be. No hard feelings, just friends clearing the air."

Melanie got to her feet and took several steps away from Salvani, ignoring his effort to embrace her. "Get out of my house at once," she said through tight lips.

"Melanie, for pity's sake," Harris muttered. "You're being very rude."

"It's all right, I understand," Salvani said, exuding good nature. "I'm to blame for the misunderstanding, and I've come to apologize. What a fool I was to frighten you! I forgot how hysterical women can be. How can I make amends?"

"You can't," Melanie said angrily. "But if you were to leave right now, it would save me the trouble of having you thrown out."

Salvani gave a slight shrug. His face was a mask of saintly endurance. "Perhaps this wasn't such a good idea, after all," he said to Harris. "I ought to do as the lady says, and leave."

"You'll do no such thing," Harris insisted. He took Melanie's hands. "Please, darling, don't make a scene."

She shook herself free, her eyes blazing. "I'll never forgive you for this," she said. "I wouldn't have dreamed you could be so stupid and insensitive, but perhaps I *should* have known. Perhaps it's been staring me in the face all these years and I never noticed. Anyway, I've discovered now. I'll say just this to you, Harris. This man is no guest of mine and I want him off my property." She turned to Salvani. "Understand, once and for all, that I'll *never* sell Terrafiore to you. You're wasting your time."

She gave them one last furious look before escaping from the room as quickly as she could.

Nine

As Melanie reached her bedroom she stopped, certain that she'd heard a noise from the next corridor, which was unused. Frowning, she headed for the corner, but before she reached it Zenia came hurrying around and nearly collided with her. Zenia stopped abruptly and turned a deathly color at the sight of Melanie. "What were you doing there?" Melanie asked.

Zenia's eyes flickered wildly from side to side before she managed to stammer, "Cleaning, *padrona.*"

"Cleaning? At this hour? Besides, you clean along there on Tuesday mornings."

"But I—I didn't do it properly last time," Zenia said frantically, "so I went back to do it again."

"Stop being absurd. What are you really doing?"

"Nothing *padrona.* I—I keep some of my things in one of the rooms...."

It was a reasonable explanation, and if Zenia had offered it at the start, Melanie would have accepted it. But by now her suspicions were aroused. Despite their brief truce over the blouse, she knew Zenia meant her no good, and if there was a secret she'd be safer knowing it. "I'm going to look," she said.

Zenia made a frantic effort to bar her way, and when she failed, hurried along beside her, wailing, "I beg you, don't go any farther. It's nothing to do with you, I swear it."

Melanie had stopped in the corridor, unsure which room to enter. As she stood there, a faint noise reached her ears. It came from behind the door nearest her and was unmistakably the sound of a man breathing. A terrible suspicion tore through her. Zenia would stop at nothing. "Who is behind that door, Zenia?" she asked in a carefully controlled voice.

"Nobody, *padrona,* I swear it."

"You're lying," Melanie said coldly, "and I'm not going to be deceived."

Ignoring Zenia's little shriek of protest, Melanie stepped up to the door and flung it open. Then she stopped on the threshold, riveted by the sight of the young man and woman standing there, clutched protectively in each other's arms, both half-naked and clearly terrified. It was Franco, Salvani's meek son-in-law, and Lucia.

"Oh, heavens!" Melanie exclaimed involuntarily.

Zenia hurried into the room and quickly closed the door. "So now you know," she said. "This is my friend, Lucia. They are in love," she added passionately, as though Melanie had argued. "They would have married if Franco hadn't been such a spineless fool." The young man shuffled his feet and didn't try to contest this view of himself, but Lucia enfolded him protectively in her arms.

"I let them come here to be together, because they have nowhere else," Zenia said. "We didn't know Salvani was going to turn up tonight." She glared challengingly at Melanie. "And now I suppose you'll go downstairs and tell him what you've discovered."

Franco whimpered with terror at the thought. Melanie had a shrewd idea of how he would be treated if she betrayed them. She shook her head. "I won't give you away," she said. "But Franco had better go quickly now, to avoid Salvani."

"Grazie, signorina," said the man fervently. *"Grazie, grazie…"*

"Shut up and be off," Zenia told him in exasperation.

"How will they get out?" Melanie asked.

"There's a back stair that leads to the work yard, past the olive press," Zenia told her. "As long as Salvani remains in the main part of the house, it's safe enough."

"Wait a moment," Melanie told her. She slipped out of the room and went to the top of the stair, where she could hear Salvani and Harris still talking below. She crept back and signaled to Zenia that the coast was clear. A moment later she saw Franco and Lucia slip out into the dark corridor and melt into the shadows to the rear of the house. She was full of pity for the two young people who had become victims of Salvani's greed, as she might have become herself but for Vittorio.

Salvani drove away half an hour later. Soon afterward Melanie heard Harris's footsteps on the stairs and waited for him in her bedroom doorway. "We've got to talk," she said.

"Yes, I should think we have. That was a nice performance you put on for Salvani when he was only trying to be helpful. I've told him to return later."

"If he sets foot on this property again I shall have him thrown off," Melanie said flatly. "He doesn't belong here, and neither do you, Harris. I think you should go back to England as soon as possible."

"Not until you come with me."

"I'll come when I'm good and ready—if I ever am. In the meantime, I want you to leave. As long as you're here, Salvani thinks he has a chance of persuading me."

"You'd actually be mad enough to stay here?" he said incredulously.

"For the moment I'm staying, yes. If that's madness, I can't help it."

"And what about us?"

"There isn't any 'us,'" she said simply. "I'm sorry, Harris, I should have refused you a long time ago, but I've only just discovered the truth about myself."

He stared at her, baffled, then began to pace about the room. "I don't understand you," he said at last. "I've told you I'm prepared to overlook your little fling. All I ask is that you get it in perspective yourself."

She looked at him curiously. She'd always known that Harris was a moderate man in his emotions as in everything else, but this had never struck her as strange until now, when the revelation of true passion had burst on her like a thunderclap, and Vittorio's tormented words, "the thought of you with another man..." still rang in her ears. Now she understood that Harris's "love" for her wasn't what she thought of as love at all.

"Go home, Harris," she said. "You'll find someone suitable to be Lady Brennan, someone who sees life in the same way."

"As you do," he insisted stubbornly.

"As I used to, as I never can again."

Suddenly he stopped in front of her and seized her in his arms, pressing his lips hard against hers with a gesture of abandon. But it was all false, as she realized at once. He was indulging her with an appearance of the romantic intensity he thought she wanted, but it was a travesty, coming from his head not his heart. Melanie didn't protest, but stood still, waiting for him to accept the inevitable.

And then she thought she heard a soft rumble, so faint that she had to strain to be sure. "Listen," she said intently.

"I don't hear anything," he said, trying to kiss her again.

But she broke free and ran to the window, looking up to the summit where she could see the glow of Etna. It looked no brighter or bigger then usual, and yet she was filled with foreboding. "It's the mountain, I'm sure of it," she said intently.

"Now I suppose you're going to tell me the mountain's angry, or some such peasant nonsense," Harris said sardonically. "You're getting as superstitious as they are."

"You should be glad to see the back of all of us then," she said. "Please go, Harris. It's for the best."

"All right, I'll leave tomorrow, and if you have any sense you'll come back with me to where you belong, and not be deluded by something that isn't real and can't last."

"It lasted for Dulcie," she flung at him.

"You don't know that. She probably regretted her marriage a million times, but was too proud to admit it.

I only hope you don't discover your mistake when it's too late."

They no longer had anything important to say to each other, so she let him go without another word. But everything in her protested at his cynicism. What she shared with Vittorio felt as fierce and everlasting as the fertile, dangerous land. Vittorio was part of that land, as it was part of him, and increasingly Melanie, too, felt at one with it. She knew now why Dulcie had abandoned her genteel security in England to live amid this savage beauty with the man she loved.

She saw Harris off at the airport next day. He kissed her cheek, said, "I'll be waiting," and walked away. As soon as he was out of sight, she hurried back to Terrafiore, and it felt like coming home.

Zenia met her as she entered the house. "Your friend has gone?" she asked.

"Yes, he's gone back to England, and he won't be returning," Melanie said.

"And you?" Zenia demanded with a touch of defiance.

Melanie's lips tightened. She didn't care for being interrogated by Zenia, but she said, "I shall be staying here. Sir Harris's visit was useful, because it showed us that we don't suit each other. So whoever sent for him did me a favor."

Zenia's eyes widened with dismay. "And you are going to stay at Terrafiore?"

"Since it belongs to me, I shall stay if I wish," Melanie informed her. "Now I've answered enough of your questions. Did your friends escape all right?"

"Yes, they were quite safe," Zenia replied, adding sullenly, "thank you." Her manner was confused.

The thought of Vittorio still hung between them, and it was clear to Melanie that Zenia didn't know whether to show her gratitude or dislike. "I can't understand how he could have married one woman if he loved another," she said.

"Because it wasn't enough for him to be rich," Zenia retorted caustically. "He wanted to be a 'big man' as well. Men do what they have to if there's something they want—even make love to women they don't care for. They all do it." She looked at Melanie significantly. *"Be warned."*

Melanie faced her, refusing to be intimidated by the implication. "You're wrong," she said firmly. "Some men may be like that, but not all."

"All men," Zenia insisted with a glint in her eye. "One woman for love and another woman for necessity, but the woman for love is the one who matters. A man wants a woman who turns to fire in his arms, not a pallid milk-and-water lady." She ran away before Melanie could answer.

Melanie went up to change into her riding things. The house was quiet as she came downstairs into the yard. It was Sunday, and most of the household had gone to church. Next day they would begin fetching in the harvest, and this was their last chance to rest before the big labor. She saddled Rosa herself and rode out, glad of the chance to be alone with her thoughts.

Zenia's malicious hint echoed in her brain despite her attempts to dismiss it. She'd lain ecstatically in Vittorio's arms and been sure in her heart that they were equal in passion. And yet—suppose the fulfillment she thought so complete was but a pale shadow of the Sicilian fire that was born in him and that he wanted in a woman? Suppose there was another dimension, denied to her but which he knew, a dimension that a "pallid milk-and-water lady" could never discover? She tried to push her fears away, but they crept back into her mind with subtle, insidious movements.

She came out of her reverie to discover that she'd wandered up the mountain, near to the path that led to Vittorio's cottage. Rosa took it automatically and Melanie made no effort to turn the mare back. Her heart yearned to be with him, to see how he would look at her and hear what he would say when she told him that Harris had gone.

At last she came around a high clump of rocks to where she could see his cottage. At once she reined Rosa in with a sharp movement and sat there motionless, watching uneasily.

Zenia was also heading for the cottage. She was just up ahead, with her back to Melanie, skimming over the rough ground with the ease of a mountain goat. But her appearance told a different story. She was wearing the luxurious peacock-blue blouse, and her hair was more carefully dressed than Melanie had ever seen it, giving her beauty a new dimension of sophistication.

She hastened up the path to the cottage door and knocked eagerly. After a moment the door opened. Melanie couldn't see who was inside, but she saw the blissful smile that broke over Zenia's face. A hand appeared, a strong male hand that Melanie recognized, and it curved to welcome Zenia in. Then Zenia sped inside and the door closed behind her.

Melanie stayed quite still, unable to move, telling herself to be sensible. Vittorio and Zenia had known each other for years. She must have visited him here a thousand times. But her mind's eye saw the blouse, the carefully arranged hair. Zenia had adorned herself like a young woman going to an assignation with her lover.

Melanie urged the mare away, anxious to be gone from here before one of them looked out and saw her. She headed farther up, not caring where she was going.

Soon she was high enough to see the streaks of lava that lay like black fingers down the side of the mountain. The air was cooler here, and there was a sudden feeling of bleakness that lay like a weight on her heart.

And then the scenery changed unexpectedly as Rosa found her way into a small gully. Its walls rose on either side, made from lava, and between them lay a carpet of flowers like none Melanie had ever seen before. She dismounted and stooped to look at them closely, wondering at their beauty in the midst of so much barrenness. She held one between her fingers. The leaves were dark with a strange ridged pattern. The flowers were nearly six inches across, and at first glance the petals seemed white, but near the center there appeared a pink tinge that shaded into deepest red at the flower's heart.

Then she remembered Vittorio saying she was a fire flower, white but with a heart of flame. These beautiful blooms must be fire flowers. As she looked, a strange thing happened. Gradually the weight on her heart seemed to lift. The unexpected beauty, coming when she most needed something to lighten her spirits, was like the flooding of light to welcome her home. She understood now that she loved this place too much ever to want to leave it. Sicily and Terrafiore were turning her into a new person; she was discovering depths in herself that she hadn't dreamed existed. And now it was as though the land had told her that it wanted her to stay.

She smiled at the thought, realizing that she'd fallen into Vittorio's ways of looking at things. If he was here now, she would tell him. There was earth on her hands, the black earth of Terrafiore. Vittorio had said it would never belong to her until she loved it, and today she'd earned the right to it. She inhaled its odor of sulphur and rich fertility and realized that the last time she had inhaled such a joyful scent had been when she held Vittorio's body to her at the moment of fulfillment. He was part of the earth and it was part of him, and it seemed simple and inevitable that to love one was to love the other.

Once she would have tried to analyze her feelings, trying to separate her love for the man from her love for the land he had revealed to her. But she was wiser now and knew that questions were foolish and meaningless. She swung herself back up into the saddle, eager to go to Vittorio, no longer afraid.

On her way back down the mountain, she found herself looking at the most breathtaking view she'd ever seen. It stretched for miles, the clear air showing her details at an incredible distance. She could make out a herd of wild horses galloping freely, led by an animal whose black coat gleamed in the sun. She wondered if it was the stallion that she always thought of as hers—hers and Vittorio's, but it was too far to be sure.

She stopped for a moment to drink in the wild beauty, and from somewhere nearby she was sure she heard a faint melancholy sound. She listened intently and heard it again, a plaintive whinnying. A little farther on, a sudden drop in the land showed her the answer. A mare lay motionless on the ground, and beside it, nudging his mother in apparent bewilderment, was a foal. A quick glance showed Melanie that the mare was recently dead. Her long-legged foal looked only a few days old, far too young to survive alone, and there were no other animals in sight.

Melanie caressed the little creature's ears abstractedly, wondering what she could do for it. Back home in England she would have been in command, but in this fierce landscape, she needed help. "Vittorio," she said at last, unconsciously speaking aloud. "This is his land. He'll know what to do."

She gently persuaded the foal away from its dead mother, and it followed her with apparent trust. When she reached Rosa, she managed to lift it across her saddle, then mounted behind it and began to make her way back down to the cottage.

At last the huge rock with the little dwelling on top came into sight, and at once, Melanie saw what she would rather not have seen—Zenia running down the mountainside, not looking back. Melanie waited until she was out of sight before approaching Vittorio's door. She knocked and entered at once. Vittorio was in the shadows and she couldn't see him properly, but she had an impression that he turned quickly away when he saw her and rubbed the back of his hand against his mouth. But with her thoughts on the foal, she barely registered what she'd seen. "Is anything wrong?" he asked.

"I need your help." She explained about the dead mare and at once he hurried down the path to where she'd left the foal. He didn't ask what she expected him to do. He accepted it as natural, just as she had found it natural to bring a frightened, orphaned creature to him.

"Poor little fellow," he murmured. "What did the mare look like?"

"Gray with a white star on her forehead."

"I think I know her. She's quite old. Probably giving birth was too much for her. So now he's my responsibility.'' He patted the foal soothingly, but it struggled out of his arms and made its way back to Melanie, pushing its soft nose insistently against her. Vittorio grinned. ''You were the one who took him from his mother, so he's adopted you instead.''

She smiled. ''I think he's hungry.''

''Then let's get some milk into him before I take him where he'll be safe.''

He produced a jug of strong-smelling goat's milk and warmed it up slightly. Melanie scooped a little into the palm of her hand and the foal drank it eagerly. Bit by bit she persuaded him to drink all the milk and waited while he licked her fingers. When she looked up, she found Vittorio watching her with a curious expression that she'd never seen on his face before. Then he seemed startled, as though she'd caught him off guard, and said quickly, ''Now I'll take him to his new home.''

''Where's that?''

''A little corral I've built about half a mile away. I've found orphaned foals before, and what they mostly need is some peace and quiet in a safe place, and regular feeding. Luckily, there'll be company for him. There's an elderly mare and a couple of horses that got left behind by the herd. That's nature's way, so it's probably perverse of me to keep them alive, but I like having them around.'' He pulled gently on the foal's ears. ''At least he won't be alone. You can leave him with me now.''

''I'm coming with you,'' she said at once.

The three of them walked the first part of the way, then the foal seemed to tire and Vittorio picked it up in his arms and carried it. At last the corral came into sight. It was a pleasant place, with some light wooden fences built around a few shady trees and a tiny stream running through. The animals whinnied in delight when they saw

Vittorio approaching, and ambled over to welcome him. He set the foal down and stood back, giving them all a chance to become acquainted. The two horses ignored the baby, and the mare seemed suspicious at first, but then she strolled slowly over to the stream and began to drink from it. After a moment the foal followed her example. "They'll be all right," Vittorio said, smiling.

Melanie didn't answer. She was looking at him, thinking that he presented a mystery to which she might never know the answer. But she knew this. Wherever Vittorio was, there was life. Those powerful yet strangely gentle hands were skilled in coaxing life from the soil or restoring it to sick and weary creatures. He had brought her heart to life, driving out the dull acceptance that had been there before, giving her instead a burning awareness of all the good things of the world, of which he was the best. And she promised herself that one day soon, they would make new life between them.

They went down the mountain together and when they came to the island, he took her hand and led her into the cottage. "Has he gone?" he asked her when the door was closed.

"Yes, I saw Harris off at the airport earlier today. He won't come back here."

"And you?" He was looking at her intently.

"I'm going to stay here because—" Suddenly she had an inspiration. To tell Vittorio directly that she loved him would be to risk offending his touchy pride, but there was a way of conveying the truth obliquely, and that was to talk to him in the language he understood best.

"I'm going to stay because—Terrafiore is mine now, truly mine in the only way that counts, mine because I love it," she said. "It's what you've been trying to make me understand all the time, isn't it?—that the land is what really matters.'' She waited for the look of pleasure that she'd been sure she would see on his face, but instead he looked mysteriously troubled. ''Don't you understand what I'm telling you?'' she asked eagerly.

''I'm—not quite sure that I do,'' he said slowly.

''I'm saying that I love it as you do yourself. You showed me the way and now—now I'll never leave. I'll defend Terrafiore against Salvani or anyone else who tries to take it away from me.'' She added with a little smile, ''I know now what Dulcie knew, why she never came back to England even for a short visit. She couldn't bear to leave the love she'd found here, even for a moment.''

''And you?'' he asked after a silence. ''Are you saying that—it's the same with you?''

''Yes,'' she said gladly. ''It's exactly the same with me.'' For a moment she thought he wasn't going to move. Then he came toward her and put his hands on either side of her head, looking down intently into her face.

''Never leave me,'' he said huskily.

Ten

She answered his plea by putting her arms about him and laying her lips on his. At once he bent and lifted her, carrying her to the bedroom, where he laid her down on the bed. They were both urgent, eager to unite again, as if each were trying to allay some secret anxiety.

As he removed her clothes, he whispered, "I was afraid we'd never be like this together again."

"But it was you who said that it must be over between us," she reminded him.

"I was a fool," he said, laying his lips against her breast. "It will never be over between us. Don't you sense that, too?"

"Yes," she said, feeling the excitement begin. "Even when I was away from you, I was always with you. The world seemed so empty, and I couldn't escape the emptiness because it was inside me, and it was the lack of you."

She undid the buckle of his belt, releasing it and pulling his trousers down over his hips. He helped her, and when they were naked together, he kissed her body with feverish possessiveness, tracing her shape with his fingers while his tongue teased her soft skin.

"Where did you go?" she murmured.

"Higher up the mountain to a place where I knew you'd never find me." He laid his face against her breast. "I slept out in the open and lived rough, trying to forget the feel of your arms holding me. But you were there in the stars and the wind, and I knew I had to come back. I'll never leave you again. You're mine . . . mine. . . ."

The ardor in his voice seemed to contain a promise, and Melanie relaxed, letting the pleasure wash over her as his lips began to tease one nipple into a proud peak. Their surroundings grew hazy. The only thing that was real was this man who could make her flesh sing such sweet songs. They were from different worlds. The sight of her pale, delicate frame against his sturdy brown one proclaimed that. But the unity of their desire made one world with only one language, which only they could speak.

She traced delicate patterns on his skin, teasing him in a way she'd already learned that he liked. To her delight she could see the effect at once, and the sight started a throbbing deep within her loins. At this moment there was nothing sophisticated about what she felt for this man. She wanted him in the most basic sense, and the knowledge that he wanted her fired her on. She seized him with fierce possessiveness, making him move over her. It was an imperious action, leaving him no choice but to take her, yet he made no resistance.

When he was inside her, she gasped with pleasure and clung to him, thrusting upward against him with abandoned strength and inspiring him to greater vigor in response. It was raw, primitive desire, earthy and elemental, something that would once have been beyond the comprehension of the elegant Lady Melanie Carlyle. But she had discovered and embraced it, and it had changed her forever. When she felt the pleasure carrying her to the heights, she yielded herself to it completely, all reticence discarded, moving with him in ecstatic abandon until they took their moment together, becoming one in the furnace heat of desire fulfilled. But when she opened her eyes, she found they were two again, and there was a momentary ache of disappointment.

She slept for a while and awoke to find Vittorio gazing down into her face, with a look of such tenderness in his eyes that her heart lurched. "I've been waiting for you to awake," he said. "If you'd slept much longer my courage would have failed me."

"Courage? Why should you need courage?"

"Because I'm going to do something I once swore never to do. I'm going to ask you to be my wife."

Through her rush of joy, one question demanded to be asked. "Are you sure this is what you really want?"

"Is that your way of saying that you don't trust me?" he asked.

The picture of Zenia running away seemed to skim across the surface of her mind in the split second before she said firmly, "Of course I trust you. It's just that after some of the things I've heard you say…"

He smiled. "I've said a great deal about pride, haven't I? Once it was the most important thing in the world. Now—" He rose, went to the dresser by the window and pulled open a little drawer. From it he took a small object that he brought over to her. "See," he said, laying it gently in her hand, "I fashioned it myself, for you."

It was a ring, made out of black horsehair, woven in an intricate pattern, an exquisite piece of work. "I took the hairs from the stallion," Vittorio told her. "I wouldn't have done that for anyone but you."

She looked up at him. "When did you decide to ask me to marry you?"

A shadow of something that might have been unease flickered across his face, "Does it matter? Now is the right time," he replied. "I planned to give you this as a betrothal gift. If you're not ready, take it anyway, and when you make your decision, look at it and remember what there is between us."

She let him slip it onto her finger, but something compelled her to ask, "What is there between us?"

Vittorio shook his head. "If your heart doesn't tell you, no words of mine can do so."

She almost answered that sometimes words mattered, but the sight of the ring, so lovingly fashioned, was like a powerful magic, driving out everything but him. "I'll marry you, Vittorio" she said, pulling him down to kiss her.

"You'll never regret what you've given up for me," he said. "I swear it."

"But I'm not giving anything up. I have all I want right here."

As she was getting dressed, he said, "Tomorrow we start the harvest, and for a week we won't be able to think of anything but work. Let's wait until it's over before we tell anyone."

A little inner demon prodded her to say, "Surely we should tell Annunciata and Zenia?"

After a long silence Vittorio said heavily, "Not just for the moment."

"But surely, they're practically your family?"

"Yes, but I'd rather wait until the harvest is complete. It has to be done in the right way. Since my mother died, Annunciata has been like a second mother to me. She'll probably want to enjoy a good cry." He tried to smile at his own joke, but somehow it fell flat.

"And Zenia has always been your little sister," Melanie couldn't stop herself saying. "I saw her coming up here this afternoon, by the way." She tried to sound casual.

"Yes, she—Annunciata sent her with a message," Vittorio said.

She thrust aside the thought that Zenia must have been there for well over an hour. They were old friends. Why shouldn't they talk for a while? But she suddenly wanted to leave and be alone with her thoughts.

"Shall I see you back to the villa?" he asked, brushing his lips against her hair.

"No, I can manage. I'll see you tomorrow morning."

"Maybe not," he said with a sigh. "Harvesting will start very early, before you're awake. But perhaps you'll come out into the fields and see me?"

"Yes, I'll do that." She kissed him, and when he kissed her back, the old sweet warmth flooded over her again, promising joyous fulfillment in the years ahead if only she could banish the little nagging doubt from her mind.

On the ride home, she began to see things more sensibly. Zenia's visit was a trifle to which she was attaching far too much importance. The rush of common sense was so strong that she almost turned around and rode back, but darkness was beginning to fall. Tomorrow she would see him and know that everything was all right. She was smiling happily to herself as she finished her journey.

She arrived to find the lights of the house on and went straight into the kitchen for a drink. Zenia was there, cutting bread. To Melanie's surprise, she still wore the peacock-blue blouse. "Don't wear that for working," Melanie advised her. "It'll get damaged."

Zenia smiled insolently. "But it is already damaged—*padrona*," she said in a soft, insulting voice, turning her shoulder to demonstrate what she meant.

Melanie froze. The blouse was ripped where the sleeve joined the shoulder, as though someone had held Zenia by the arms, held her fiercely and with passionate abandon, so that the tearing of the material went unnoticed.

Stop it, she told herself fiercely. You're thinking just what she wants you to think. She could have torn that herself. But then she saw something Zenia couldn't have done to herself. The tear in the material had exposed four small red marks on her arm, marks that could only have been made by a hand, a large, powerful male hand. She noticed too that Zenia's hair had lost its careful arrangement and her lipstick was smudged, and in the same moment she remembered Vittorio quickly rubbing his hand over his mouth when she appeared.

Zenia's eyes were on her, as brilliant and all-seeing as a hawk's, reading every passing thought. They took in the slight disarray of Melanie's hair, so like her own, and the horsehair ring on her finger, and suddenly she burst into a loud, coarse laugh. Melanie stood her ground, but inwardly she was dying at the implications of that laugh.

Annunciata came hurrying into the kitchen. "Don't stand there laughing," she reproved her daughter. "Finish your work."

"In a minute, Mama," Zenia said carelessly. "First I must go and change my blouse. It got torn this afternoon." She smiled directly into Melanie's eyes and sauntered out.

Annunciata made a sound of exasperation. "That girl! She gets more unreliable every day. This afternoon she vanished for hours on end without telling me where she was going, and since she came back she's been singing and laughing to herself like a crazy woman."

So Annunciata hadn't sent Zenia to Vittorio with a message. He had lied to her. And with that realization her heart seemed to break apart.

She ate her meal like an automaton, leaving most of it untouched. Pictures danced in her head: Zenia, laughing at her and saying, "One woman for love and another for necessity, but the one for love is the one that matters;" Vittorio rubbing his mouth, lying to her about Zenia's visit. But the worst picture of all was in the future: tomorrow when she would confront him and he would lie again, soothing her with false words of love—and afterward going to Zenia.

The choice before her was simple—to let herself live in a fool's paradise, using passion as a drug to block out the mockery, or to keep her self-respect even at a terrible cost.

By the time she went up to bed, she'd made her decision and her eyes were bleak and empty.

She was up early next morning, waiting for Vittorio in the room Giorgio had once used as an office. She knew he would come to her because she'd left a message with Leo. At last she saw him from the window, crossing the yard, and she had a stab of pain at the way the sun touched his unruly hair, catching the hint of blue in the black locks that lay against the brown skin of his neck.

The pain was repeated when he appeared in the doorway, smiling at the sight of her and coming forward with his arms outstretched. "Leo gave me your message," he said. "In my heart I was expecting it. I knew we couldn't start the day without seeing each other."

Before she could retreat, he had taken her in his arms and kissed her. It took all her strength not to succumb to the insidious delight of that kiss. She wanted him so much and it would be so easy to just yield and let the future take care of itself. But she forced herself to be resolute and stiffened within his embrace.

"What is it, my love?" he asked, looking down on her.

"Let me go, Vittorio. There's something I have to say to you."

A note in her voice seemed to warn him of what was coming, for his face grew dark as he released her. "Tell me."

"I did a lot of thinking last night and—and I've decided it would be best if we didn't marry after all."

The silence that followed seemed to last forever. Then Vittorio said, "What has happened?"

She almost weakened and told him, but that would be to give him the chance to lie again, and something in her revolted at the prospect. "Nothing has happened," she said as calmly as she could. "As I say I've been thinking, and I've realized you were right about a lot of things. You said there was an unbridgeable chasm between us and—"

"But you've never believed that," he interrupted.

"I thought I didn't," she shot back quickly, "but I've come to think differently about a lot of things."

"And so have I," he said with a touch of grimness. "You persuaded me of your way of thinking, that pride is unimportant compared to what a man and a woman feel about each other. If I didn't believe that, I couldn't have asked *Lady* Melanie Carlyle to be my wife. But you convinced me. You said nothing is impossible."

"I was wrong."

He stared at her in disbelief, and a black, bitter anger dawned in his eyes. "My God," he breathed, "Are you that kind of woman?"

"I don't know what kind you mean—"

"The kind that only wants a man when she can't have him. Last night I went against everything I've always believed because you mattered more. And that was when you lost interest, wasn't it? I was right when I said I was your plaything, but now the play is played out, and you're instantly bored. Will my scalp look good on your wall, and how many others will hang beside it?"

She was silent racked with torment and indecision.

"At least have the grace to be honest," he grated.

"You can explain it any way you like," she said bleakly.

She thought he was going to explode with anger, but after a tense moment, he came closer and lifted her chin with his fingers. "No," he said somberly, "that isn't the answer. That would make everything that's been between us meaningless, and I can't—I won't believe that."

"Only the land matters," she cried. "That's what you taught me."

"But the land is worked by men and women, who must love it—but also love each other. That's what *you* taught *me.*"

She didn't answer, because she couldn't. This was a thousand times harder than she'd feared. If only it would end soon. But after gazing intently into her face with its signs of struggle, Vittorio said, "Perhaps I should remind you of your own lesson," and drew her against him before she could protest.

"Was this meaningless?" he said against her mouth, "and this…and this…?" He was raining kisses over her face as he spoke, calling up a thousand remembrances that she'd tried to kill because they would weaken her. Her body turned traitor, reliving the delight she'd always found in his embrace, that only he could give. But her heart was the bigger traitor, asking how she could endure life without him.

"Was it meaningless?" he repeated, touching her neck with feather-light caresses of his lips.

"No..." she whispered, fighting to keep control.

"And when you lay naked in my arms, wasn't it your heart that spoke to mine?" he urged.

She met his eyes. "Have you got a heart, Vittorio?"

"I don't understand you. You're talking wildly."

Using all her strength, she forced him to let her go. "On my first day here—I heard you talking about me with Zenia. You said you were afraid of doing something that would make you hate yourself."

His eyes kindled. "And what did you read into that?"

"You're Giorgio's son. We both know it. And my 'English common sense' has come back to me."

He stared at her. "And it makes you think—all this time you've suspected me?" His face was grim. "I told you once I couldn't take from you what he wouldn't give me."

"Yes, and something made you change your mind."

"I changed my mind because I thought we loved each other."

"Or was it that Harris showed you the danger?"

He was silent for a moment while his face grew pale beneath its tan. Then he took a step away from her. "Why are you determined to insult me?"

"I haven't insulted you, Vittorio. I've simply recognized that there's nothing you wouldn't do for Terrafiore."

His jaw set. "That at least is true. And what Terrafiore needs now is for its harvest to be taken in. That's more important than our private quarrels."

"Wait," she said before he could go. She held out the horsehair ring to him. He took it and held it for a moment before giving her a look that she knew she would never forget to her dying day. Then he went out without another word.

Eleven

In the week that followed, Melanie barely set eyes on Vittorio. He devoted himself entirely to the harvest, rising at the crack of dawn and often going to oversee the work without even coming to the villa. Sometimes in the evening he would speak to her briefly to make a report, but he kept his manner coolly correct and didn't meet her eyes.

On Saturday night he said, "Do you wish me to ask them to work tomorrow? It will cost more."

"No, let them have a rest. They've earned it. I'll go down to Catania." She didn't know why she told him that, unless to make it clear that she wasn't going to sit pining in the house while he spent the day with Zenia. Vittorio nodded, bid her a polite good-night and departed.

Next morning she was up early, and looking out of her window, she saw the distant figure of Zenia making her way up the mountain in the direction of Vittorio's cottage. She turned away, heartsick.

She changed her mind about Catania, and instead went out alone to look at the fields, which had been stripped of their fruits. Two-thirds of the harvest was now safely in store, and soon the rest would follow. This should have been the moment she and Vittorio shared, the moment when Terrafiore's bounty symbolized the richness of the life they would make together, but in the midst of abundance, her heart was barren. She worked hard at letting herself feel nothing, because otherwise the pain would be more than she could bear.

As she made her way slowly home, she looked up to where Etna's glow lit the sky, wondering if the nimbus really was brighter tonight or whether it was just her fancy. It was evening and the air should have been cooler, yet for some reason it was oppressively hot, and the stillness all about her had an eerie quality. She stopped and listened and realized that not a single bird broke the silence.

Then it came again, the muffled roar she'd first heard in Vittorio's arms as they lay in blissful content in his cottage. And at the same moment she felt the earth shake beneath her. Rosa whinnied and began to tremble.

"It's all right," Melanie soothed her. "It happens sometimes, but it's quite normal. *He* said so."

The sound died away to a faint murmur, and she rode on to the villa. Annunciata was standing in the courtyard when she arrived. "I hate it when it's like this," she said with a sigh. "I know it doesn't mean anything, and yet I hate it. One day it *will* mean something."

"Were you here the last time there was an eruption?" Melanie asked.

"Oh, yes, *padrona*. That was only eight years ago."
Annunciata added scathingly, "Scientists came and said
it was only a very small eruption, and we were lucky. But
even a 'small eruption' is a bad thing to live through."

In her bedroom Melanie took a last look over the
countryside in the fast-fading light. She was about to step
away from the window when she noticed something
moving toward the house at tremendous speed, and in
another moment she recognized Salvani's ostentatious
car, being driven hell-for-leather over the bumpy road.
She hurried back down at once, ready to order him off
her property, and reached the yard just as he screeched to
a halt.

Salvani hauled himself out from behind the wheel and
bore down on her, his face red and sweating. "Where are
they?" he shouted.

"Where are who?" she snapped.

"The criminals. I'll give you one chance to give them
up to me or I'll tear this place apart to find them."

"I think you must have taken leave of your senses,"
Melanie said. "I don't know what you're talking about
and I don't care."

"Don't play ignorant with me," he raged, "I know
they meet here. They've been seen leaving together. That
pig thinks he can dishonor my family and get away with
it, but I'll tear him limb from limb."

As it dawned on Melanie whom he meant, a stab of
fear went through her, not for herself, but for Franco and
Lucia, whose secret had plainly been discovered. But she
kept her head well enough to repeat firmly. "I don't
know who you're talking about." She didn't feel any ob-
ligation to give Salvani the truth.

"I'm talking about that dirty little mechanic that I allowed to join my family," Salvani yelled. "I'm talking

about the cheap woman he sleeps with. They've vanished. Nobody has seen them since last night."

"That has nothing to do with me," she said coldly.

"Of course it has. They've run here to hide and I expect them handed over."

"Do you, indeed? Then you're going to be disappointed. They're not here, and you'll get off my land *now*." She sent up a silent prayer that Franco and Lucia hadn't taken refuge at Terrafiore.

"I'm going to search your house," Salvani snapped, "and when I find them, it'll be the worse for you." He advanced on her. Melanie made frantic efforts to block his path, but he thrust her aside so roughly that she fell. He ignored her and stormed into the house.

Melanie picked herself up, her eyes blazing. But as she prepared to follow Salvani into the house, she found her way blocked by a frantic Annunciata. "Don't stop him, *padrona*," she begged. "He's a bad man to thwart."

"Did I hear you properly?" Melanie demanded, incensed. "Do you think I'm going to stand by while he raids my house? Besides—" she paused, wondering whether it would be safe to voice her concern.

But Annunciata read her expression and lowered her voice. "Don't worry," she muttered. "They're not here."

"What do you know, Annunciata?"

"Only what my daughter has told me. They have run away, far, far from here. She helped them escape. Franco is determined to get a divorce."

"Well, at least if Salvani doesn't find them here, that's something," Melanie said quietly. Above them they could hear the noise of Salvani throwing open doors and yelling with rage as he discovered nothing. "But I'm not standing for that," she added. She ran into the stables and hunted around until she found a pitchfork. "Let's see how he faces up to this," she said to Annunciata when she returned.

The older woman paled. "You will use that on him?"

"I won't need to. Just the sight of it will work a miracle. Watch me."

Annunciata shuddered. "Soon the fire flowers will appear," she whispered.

"What does that mean?"

"It means Salvani is a cruel man, and will make people suffer for his anger. In these parts, we say 'the fire flowers will bloom' when we expect trouble, because the fire flowers only bloom when the mountain is about to erupt."

In her head there was an echo of Vittorio saying that *she* was a fire flower and that it meant danger. "But what are fire flowers?" she asked.

"They grow much higher up, directly from the lava. They look white at first, but when you look closely you can see that they have fire at their heart. They're very rare, but someone sees them every few years."

A dreadful suspicion was growing in Melanie. "Are they broad flowers, with dark green leaves that have a ridged pattern?"

"That's right, *padrona*. You have seen pictures?"

"No," she said grimly, "I've seen the flowers, just where you said, high up in a lava gully."

"Merciful heaven!" Annunciata crossed herself.

"But, Annunciata, surely it's only superstition?"

"Perhaps not. I read in a book that such flowers can only grow when the earth is becoming very hot deep down, and it's the heat of the volcano that makes them appear."

"But I saw them a week ago. Nothing has happened yet."

"The book said the lava will not come until the flowers reach their full size. They grow to be very big."

"How big?" Melanie asked tensely, remembering the flowers in the gully. "Six inches?"

Annunciata nodded. "Perhaps a little more."

"Have you ever heard of anyone else seeing them?"

"Only once, and that was eight years ago."

And eight years ago Etna had erupted. It might be co-incidence, but Melanie knew she didn't dare take the chance. She dropped the pitchfork and went into the house in time to meet Salvani storming down the stairs. "Where have you hidden them?" he raged.

"Nowhere, and they don't matter now," she said impatiently. "You've got to go down to Fazzoli and warn the people there that the volcano might erupt at any moment."

He made an impatient gesture. "The mountain has been rumbling all day. Nothing will happen. This is a trick to distract me—"

"No, no, *signore,*" Annunciata interrupted. "She has seen the fire flowers, and they were big."

Salvani went a ghastly color. "When was this?"

"Several days ago," Melanie told him. "It may mean nothing, but—"

She was talking to empty air. Salvani had lunged for the door and was already squeezing himself into his car. Melanie ran after him. "You've got to warn them," she cried. "Tell everyone in Fazzoli."

He stared at her. "Yes—yes, of course. I will warn them." His jaw was set as he started up the engine, and the car shot forward so fast that Melanie had to jump back.

Annunciata went in search of Leo, who listened to her, eyes wide, then threw a nervous glance at Melanie, almost as though he thought her alien presence had brought the mountain's wrath down on them. When Annunciata told him to shift himself and pass the warning on to the other estate workers, he nodded.

"Leo—" Melanie grasped his arm before he could vanish "—where is Vittorio?"

He shook his head. "I don't know, *padrona*. No one has seen him today. Shall I look for him first?"

"No, I'll go."

She swung herself into Rosa's saddle and headed up the mountain. Now she could see clearly that the glow from the summit had a terrible brightness, and even as she looked, the ground shook beneath her and the rumble came again, louder than ever. There was no longer any doubt in her mind. Etna was rousing itself to life, and in a short time its boiling lava would come streaming down, smothering everything in its path. She had no time to be afraid. One picture tortured her: Vittorio, in Zenia's arms, so lost in passion that he was oblivious to the danger. In this moment, it didn't matter that he had betrayed her. All she cared about was to see him safe.

She urged Rosa faster up the slope until at last she could make out the island standing against the red sky, and a light in the cottage window. She jumped down and ran up the path, flinging the front door open. There was no one in the main room, and without stopping to think, she pushed open the bedroom door, ready to cry out a warning.

But the room was empty.

"Vittorio," she cried desperately, but there was no reply. It took her only a moment to ascertain that neither he nor Zenia was in the cottage.

The roar came again, loud enough to split the heavens, and as it died away, she heard something else, the distant sound of horses screaming in terror. Then she remembered the horses trapped in the corral, directly in the path of the deadly lava.

She ran out and jumped up onto Rosa's back again, but when she tried to urge her up the side of the mountain, Rosa stood rigid, shaking in fear. After trying to encourage her, Melanie gave up and dismounted. It might be madness to go ahead on foot, but she couldn't leave the animals to die.

It was only half a mile, but already the air about her was hot, burning her lungs. Heat seemed to come up from the earth, filling her with dread of what was about to happen. High above her, the mouth of Etna glowed red and yellow, blasting its fury up to the night sky. And then Melanie saw something that almost made her heart stop. Gleaming yellow fingers were already stretching down from the summit. The mountain was on fire.

She could hear the horses louder now. A few more agonizing steps, and the corral appeared, and when she saw it she nearly cried out her joy and relief. For Vittorio was there. He'd opened the gate and was trying to urge the beasts out, but by now they were scared out of their wits. Instead of running through the wide gate, they circled him, screaming with fear, ignoring his efforts to get them to safety.

And then Melanie heard a sound behind her, and turning, she saw a wonderful sight. The stallion stood, silhouetted against the glow, pawing the hot ground and calling out with long, mournful whinnies. As if at a signal, the animals in the corral ceased their circling and turned for the gate. The next moment they were thundering down the mountain, directly to the place where Melanie was standing.

She heard Vittorio cry out her name. The next moment she'd flattened herself against the rock while the horses careened madly past. She held her breath as they passed within an inch of her.

And then they were gone. And when she opened her eyes, the black stallion too had gone, and all she could hear was Vittorio's voice, calling her name in a voice full of love and terror. All around them the mountain was exploding, but she no longer knew anything about it as he reached her and encircled her in his arms.

"Melanie…Melanie…" At first he could only say her name, holding on to her fiercely, as though afraid some power would snatch her away. "Melanie…my love, you were nearly killed. What possessed you to come here?"

"I came to free the horses. I should have known you'd be here, too."

His arms tightened still more. "You came all this way, for them?"

"Not just for them. I knew this was going to happen. I saw the fire flowers. I went to the cottage to warn you."

He looked down into her face. "Even though you hate me?"

"I don't hate you," she cried passionately. "I couldn't bear it if you were killed."

Before he could answer, there was a sound like an explosion higher up. "Hurry, we haven't much time," he said urgently.

Seizing her hand, he began to run back down the slope. Melanie managed to glance over her shoulder and nearly cried out, for the gleaming streams of lava looked hideously close. She stumbled but Vittorio pulled her up and raced on, her hand clasped firmly in his. She was dizzy from the heat of the air burning her lungs: her limbs ached, but there was no time to stop for rest. The lava was gaining on them, and when she thought of the distance to the bottom, she realized they could never make it.

"Vittorio," she cried.

"Just a little farther," he shouted, fixing his arm firmly around her waist. "We're nearly there."

She lost track of details. The whole mountain seemed to have turned into one brilliant furnace glow. She only knew that she was with Vittorio, her hand clasped in his, and that as long as he held her she was safe. It made no sense, but now her instincts had taken over from her head, and they told her what she should have recognized all the time, that he was a man to be trusted. If all the world seemed against him, that was only a reason for trusting him more, and it was a terrible irony that she should have learned that lesson too late.

And then she felt herself climbing and realized that they'd reached the island, and he was almost dragging her up the path to the front door. At the very moment he slammed it behind them, the gleaming fingers of red-hot lava hit the rock with an audible hiss, enclosed it and flowed on, leaving them high up, stranded but safe.

But they no longer knew or cared. They were in each other's arms.

Twelve

Their kiss was an affirmation, not only of love but of faith. Standing in his arms in the midst of danger and destruction, Melanie knew she had come home forever.

When he could speak, Vittorio said, "I thought you were in Catania, or I'd have come for you first. I nearly went mad when I saw you on the mountain, straight in the path of those horses. Thank God, you're safe!" He took a shuddering breath. "I couldn't bear life without you. I love you so." She looked up at him and he said quickly, "I know you don't believe me, but—"

"But I do believe you," she said simply. "I didn't for a while, because of Zenia, but I know now I must have been wrong. Whatever the explanation is, it can't be the one I was afraid of."

He was looking at her in total bewilderment. "What do you mean—because of Zenia?"

"I thought you were with her today. I saw her coming up here early this morning."

"But she only stayed for a moment. She was in a strange mood. She kept coming to the edge of saying goodbye and then backing off. She hadn't said anything definite by the time she went, but I have a feeling we won't find her there when we go down."

Melanie looked intently into his face. "Why should she go?"

"Darling, you must understand, I've always loved Zenia as my little sister and I still do, but she wants another kind of love from me, one that I can't give her. It took her a while to accept that, but she understands now."

"I thought there was something between you. That day I found the foal, and Zenia had been here, you said Annunciata had sent her with a message, but I know she didn't. Annunciata didn't know where she was that afternoon."

Vittorio groaned. "That'll teach me to invent stories, even small ones. When you asked me about her visit, I had to think of something quickly." He searched Melanie's face. "And you thought she and I were lovers? Never, my darling. It was something else that brought her here, something I needed time to think about."

"Can you tell me now?"

"I think I must. It's not going to be easy but—" He stopped and seemed overcome with awkwardness. "I'd better just show you," he said at last, "and we can talk about it afterward."

He went into his bedroom and rummaged through a drawer. Melanie followed him, frowning, wondering what could possibly have happened to trouble him so much. At last he put a sheet of paper into her hand. "Before you read it," he said, "I want you to promise that nothing will make any difference between you and me."

"But how could it?"

"You'll understand when you've read that paper. It changes everything. But it mustn't change *us*. Promise me that."

"I promise."

It was a short document, in scrawling handwriting, and with two signatures at the bottom. But it was Dulcie's name that caught her attention. She read slowly down the page, and as she did so, her heart began to pound as the incredible facts became clear to her.

The paper was a makeshift will, signed by Giorgio Benetto on the day of his death. In it he bequeathed Terrafiore jointly to his wife, Dulcie, and his natural son, Vittorio Farnese, with a proviso that, on Dulcie's death, her half should pass to Vittorio. The will was signed in a shaky hand witnessed by Annunciata.

Melanie read it three times and stared into space, trying to come to terms with what she'd discovered. Here it was, the natural, inevitable truth. She was an impostor. She had never been anything else. And Vittorio had known.

"*Why?*" she cried. "Why did you keep this hidden. Why deceive me and play out this farce?"

"But don't you understand? I never deceived you. I've only known myself for the past few days. This is why Zenia came here that day, to give it to me."

"But—how—I don't understand?"

He took both her hands in his and drew her down until they were both sitting on the bed. "Giorgio died of a heart attack. Dulcie was away and there was only Annunciata and Zenia in the house. He'd never made a proper will, so he scribbled out his intentions while he still had the strength, and Annunciata witnessed it. But before Annunciata could give it to anyone—'' Vittorio stopped uneasily ''—Zenia—took charge of it—''

"You mean she stole it?'' Melanie asked shrewdly.

"Well, whatever. Zenia took possession of it and wouldn't give it back. Somehow she persuaded Annunciata to keep quiet, too.''

"But why should Zenia want to do you harm?''

"She didn't see it that way. She fancied she was in love with me. It was about the same time as Franco won the lottery and jilted Lucia, and Zenia was afraid that I'd become proud, too, too proud to marry her. But I'm no weakling like Franco. If I'd loved Zenia no inheritance would have made me turn away from her, but I never loved her.'' He looked closely into her eyes. "There was nothing between us but her imagination—then or now.''

She let him draw her against him. "But I don't understand about Annunciata.'' She sighed. "How could she agree?''

"Annunciata adores her daughter and she's rather afraid of her. It wouldn't be hard for Zenia to get her own way. Besides, once she'd seized the will and refused to return it, Annunciata couldn't speak out without incriminating her. So she gave in and hoped for the best.''

"And Zenia would have seen you deprived of your rights all your life? In the name of love?''

"Not all my life. She was a little incoherent, but I think her idea was that once we were safely married the will would be miraculously 'discovered.' It was an absurd idea, for how would Annunciata explain that she'd never mentioned it before? But I don't think Zenia ever considered any of the practical aspects. She acted on impulse, and realized the problems when it was too late.''

"But she finally gave it to you?"

"Yes. She was jealous of you, and she produced the will in a last hope of separating us. She spoke as though I only wanted you for your property. She said that once Terrafiore was mine I wouldn't have to bother with you anymore. I tried to make her understand that I loved you, but she wouldn't listen. She even—" Vittorio stopped and reddened slightly. "She even put her arms around me, kissed me and tried to get me to make love to her. I pushed her away. She didn't want to let go and I'm afraid I was more rough than I meant to be, and her blouse got torn. What she'd told me about Terrafiore was almost secondary. What really shocked me was that she thought she could make me leave you—that I could love anyone but you."

He held her tightly and for a moment, she clung to him. "But when I came here later that afternoon, why didn't you tell me that Terrafiore was yours?" Melanie asked when she could speak.

"I didn't know how to. It was so much to take in. I wanted to wait and tell you in the right way. Then you came to me that day and told me how you felt about the land. You spoke of Terrafiore almost as a woman speaks of a lover, and I discovered, to my horror, that I was jealous."

He frowned as if he were searching for the words to say something important. "I'd never known a feeling like the one that afflicted me at that moment. I'd thought jealousy was what I'd felt about the Englishman, but that was nothing to what I felt when you spoke of Terrafiore with such tenderness. I heard you voicing my own thoughts, saying that the earth was more important than anything else. How often had I said such things to you? And I discovered in that moment that I no longer be-

lieved them, that there was something more important—
the love I felt for you and wanted you to feel for me. I
almost hated Terrafiore because it seemed to mean more
to you than I did.

"I became afraid that if I told you about the will, and
then asked you to marry me, you would accept me only
to stay here. So I waited, hoping to make you prove your
love by marrying me before you found out. I was a fool
to demand proof. Love is, or it is not. No man has the
right to impose tests. Forgive me, beloved."

She scarcely heard the last words. She was looking into
Vittorio's eyes, trying to understand the miraculous thing
he had said. "You love me—more than Terrafiore?" she
breathed, hardly daring to ask.

"More that the world. Tell me that you love me, and
that *is* the world for me."

"I love you," she said simply. "I didn't mean what I
said when I broke it off. I was hurt because I thought
you'd made love with her. I saw her torn blouse and the
marks on her arm, and she went out of her way to make
sure I thought the worst."

"I'm not defending Zenia, darling, but don't be too
hard on her. But for her, we would never have met."

She sighed happily. "That's true. We owe her a great
deal."

"Before you came here, I was afraid I would hate you
for taking what I felt should be mine, but I soon knew
that my love for you left no room for hate. To me you've
always been the fire flower, beautiful and delicate to look
at, but portending danger. The first moment I saw you,
looking so pale and English, I felt that your appearance
was deceptive, that behind that queenly exterior you were
as fiery as the wildest Sicilian. When I held you in my
arms, I knew I'd been right. You were a fire flower wait-

ing to be plucked, and no danger on earth could have stopped me—" he took the paper out of her hands and laid it aside "—just as nothing is going to stop me now."

He held her for a long moment before laying her back on the pillows. "I will pluck you and wear you against my heart for always," he said huskily. "And you must bloom for no man but me. Promise me that."

"Come here," she whispered, "and I will promise."

She gave him a silent promise with her lips, and his own lips returned it a thousandfold. The doubts and suspicions that had threatened their love were finally swept away. The lava enclosing them on all sides had made the cottage truly an island, cut off from the world. Yet that little space *was* the whole world to two people who were rediscovering each other.

She threw her clothes off quickly, and he did the same, for they had no more need of fears and pretenses. They knew now that their love was stronger than passion, and it was that very knowledge that gave their passion freedom to be honest. Vittorio pressed her back against the pillows and looked down on her with eyes filled with wonder. His hands were gentle as he caressed her, the fingers subtle in their loving understanding of her body. She gave a sigh of pleasure and surrendered herself willingly to their skill.

He rained small kisses on her neck with lips that burned. Ripples of excitement went through her as she felt him linger over the hollow of her throat before descending slowly to the swelling softness of her breasts. All her skin was sensitized in eager anticipation of his touch, and it took no more than the lightest flick with his tongue against one nipple to make it peak proudly. She gasped as he began to love it, teasing it softly back and forth with his tongue, making whorls on her skin.

"You are so beautiful," he whispered, "my lovely fire flower...flowering only in my arms...I want all of you."

"I've belonged to you from the first moment," she whispered back. "I shall belong to you forever."

For answer, he took her hand and laid a reverent kiss on the palm, then pressed it over his breast. "There...always."

He parted her thighs and moved over her. Her blood raced as she awaited his entry, and when it came, she cried out with ecstasy, folding her legs about him with a fierceness that was almost violent. She wanted him and she was going to have him. It was as simple and as primitive as that. Looking up at his face above her, she saw him smile, as though he'd understood the possessive power that had driven her and was pleased by it.

He moved strongly inside her pushing her closer to the edge of delirium with every thrust. Body, heart and soul, he had invaded and filled her completely, driving out everything else, and she was happy to have it so. There was nothing else in space or time but this love that had claimed them both, uniting them yet making each of them more themselves. As the pleasure rose to new heights, her understanding of this perfect wisdom grew also, so that their moment seemed to make her one with the whole universe, and its gifts were showered on her.

When she felt it all taken away, she wept a little, but he was there, promising by his presence that the blessing would be renewed. She had only to reach out for him, forever. And when she realized that, she slept in his arms.

They awoke at dawn to find a wasteland all about them. Wherever they looked, they saw smoking lava, black on the surface but with an occasional red-hot gleam discernible.

"Now you know why this is called 'the island,'" Vittorio told her. "Luckily, we have enough provisions to last while we're trapped."

"If only I could be sure that the others were safe, I could happily be trapped here alone with you forever."

"With the early warning you gave them, they should have had time to escape." He sighed. "But Terrafiore hasn't escaped. We got most of the harvest in, but some will be lost. Your olive groves will be destroyed, and it will take years to build Terrafiore back to its old magnificence."

"But we'll do it," she said. "And don't call them my olive groves. They belong to you. The will says so."

"The will means nothing to me, except as proof that my father finally acknowledged me," he said seriously. "I can't make a claim without incriminating Annunciata."

"Then I'll give Terrafiore to you as a wedding present," she insisted.

"You can give me half. I won't take more." His eyes were suddenly filled with his rare humor. "Then, if I'm a bad husband to you, you can leave and force me to buy you out. That will keep me up to the mark."

"I'm not afraid of that," she said joyfully. "I know other ways of keeping you up to the mark. Come here and I'll show you one of them."

Laughing, he went into her arms.

On their second evening, Melanie sat looking out of the window, watching the sun fade over the black landscape. "Do you think the herd of wild horses escaped?" she brooded.

"They're bound to," he reassured her. "They can go so much faster than the lava. Even the weak ones from the corral will have had a good chance."

"He came for them, you know."

"You mean the stallion?"

"Yes, that's why he was there, to give them courage and show them the way."

"Of course. He is their king, their father, their protector."

"And we'll never try to catch him, will we?"

"Never," he promised.

It was three days before Vittorio reckoned it was safe to venture out. He went first, laying his hand tentatively on the black skin that covered the earth. "It's cool," he said. "We can go down safely."

They made their way slowly on foot, looking around them at the devastation. Everywhere, they saw blackness and heard only a silence like the grave. But while Melanie's heart sank, she noticed that Vittorio was looking relieved. "It was a minor eruption," he said in answer to her query. "See how thin the lava is already. It can't have gone very far down. With luck there won't be any casualties. It depends on whether anyone managed to warn Fazzoli in time."

At that moment, Vittorio pointed down the mountain at some tiny figures who'd just come into view. He waved and one of them waved back, letting out a yell of delight. "It's Leo," Vittorio said.

Taking her hand, he began to run, and soon they met up with Leo and some of the men from Terrafiore. "We were coming up to look for you," Leo yelped, thumping him joyfully on the back. "We were afraid you would both be dead."

"What about Fazzoli?" Melanie asked.

"Everyone's safe," Leo said. "One or two of the lads went down there to tell them, but they already knew because of Salvani."

"You mean he actually warned people?" Melanie asked.

Leo cackled cheerfully. "In a way. He didn't say anything, just rushed for his own house and grabbed his valuables. The whole family cleared out. They piled two cars with luggage and drove off hell for leather, with Salvani shrieking, 'Faster, faster, the volcano will kill us.' The whole town saw him and realized what was wrong.

"They all evacuated, but the lava only touched a few houses before it stopped altogether. It made a nice mess of Salvani's house. Pity he wasn't in it, but at least it'll be a long time before he'll dare show his face here again."

The lava had reached the villa, but the tough outer walls had held, keeping the inside safe. Melanie was relieved to find Rosa, who'd made her own way home. After she'd made a fuss over her, she did a little exploring to see if an idea she'd had was feasible. She discovered that the stable had once been much larger. Zeus and Rosa now occupied one end, and the rest was empty. Melanie looked it over and nodded with satisfaction. Once a wall had been built enclosing the small stable, the rest would be an ideal location for her kiln and equipment. She could run her business just as easily from Terrafiore as from England, and the new setting would add a whole new dimension to her creativity. With her mind at ease, she went to join Vittorio.

He was in the house, trying to persuade Annunciata to come down and talk to him. When she finally appeared, it was obvious that she knew Zenia had showed him the will. She looked at him with ashamed eyes, but her shame turned to astonishment when he put his arms around her and gave her a warm hug. "It's all right," he assured her. "Everything's going to be fine."

"But I betrayed you," she said wretchedly. "I haven't known how to live with myself...and now..." She looked uncertainly at Melanie, then straightened her shoulders. "I am ready to go to the police whenever you wish," she said firmly.

"There's no need to bring in the police," Vittorio said at once. "This will remain between us."

"We're going to be married," Melanie told her.

Annunciata looked from one to the other and burst into tears. Vittorio hugged her again. "Where's Zenia?" he asked.

"She's gone," Annunciata said huskily, wiping her eyes. She brought out a letter from her pocket and handed it to Melanie. "She left this for you."

Melanie opened it and read:

I expect by now you know what I did. I don't suppose it makes any difference to you, because you will marry him. He told me he had no love to spare for me, because it was all given to you. I make no excuses. All's fair in love and war. I fought you and I lost.

I've taken your advice and gone away. I shall follow Franco and Lucia to Rome. Lucia's cousin is housekeeper for a lawyer, and he will tell Franco how to get a divorce. I shall try to be a model.

I'll need decent clothes so I've taken yours. You shouldn't grudge me a few of your possessions. You have everything that matters.

                                        Zenia.

Melanie put the letter down, feeling sorry for Zenia and yet glad that she had found another path for her life to take.

She saw Vittorio looking at her, a question in his eyes, and showed him the letter. It was true. She had all that mattered, in the earth that would need so much loving care to restore it, and in the man whose arms were going about her now, holding her close in an embrace that would last a lifetime.

* * * * *

Silhouette Desire

COMING NEXT MONTH

WARRIOR
Elizabeth Lowell

Book three of the Western Lovers Series!

Nevada Blackthorn was born of a warrior breed and he believed in survival. He sought refuge from his past on the Rocking M and couldn't believe in the love offered by Eden Summers.

CELESTIAL BODIES
Laura Leone

Private eye Nick Tremain wasn't sure if Diana and Felix Stewart were charlatans or just harmless kooks. Whichever it was, he was happy to keep an eye on the sexy redhead, but how was he going to keep a professional distance?

ROUGH PASSAGE
Paula Detmer Riggs

Regan Delaney was relieved she wasn't trapped alone in a raging forest fire; Jake Cutter felt differently. Alone he could have made it to safety easily, now both their lives were at risk.

COMING NEXT MONTH

FOR KEEPS
Donna Carlisle

When she'd agreed to look after her sister's pet-sitting agency, Lyn had no idea what she was taking on. She certainly wouldn't have believed that a dog would shut her in a cupboard with a nearly naked man!

FRAME-UP
Jessica Barkley

In the past, Cassandra Malone had made a point of keeping vet Jarrod Fitzgerald at arm's length. But now she needed his help if she was going to prove her late father's innocence.

THE DRIFTER
Joyce Thies

September's *Man of the Month*, rancher Jesse Hubbard, had no intention of allowing a luscious city slicker and her two boys to take over the land he loved. But why did Terry Brubacker have to have a body made for sin?